YOUNG BLACK STALLION

3

The Homecoming

Steven Farley

Random House 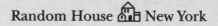 New York

To Mom and Dad

A Random House Book
Copyright © 1999 by Steven Farley
Cover art copyright © 1999 by Joanie Schwarz
Photo of girl and horse by Jane Feldman

www.randomhouse.com/kids
Library of Congress Catalog Card Number: 98-067188
ISBN: 0-679-89358-X (trade) — ISBN: 0-679-99358-4 (lib. bdg.)
RL: 4.5

Printed in the United States of America
10 9 8 7 6 5 4 3 2 1

Contents

CHAPTER ONE

Vacation

Danielle Conners watched from the grass as the little black horse surveyed the green fields of his kingdom. For a moment he remained still, blinking, his ears pricked. He looked like a statue, arrogant and noble. His finely drawn head was set majestically on his long, arching neck, and his body was perfectly molded.

A cool breeze tousled the young stallion's long black foretop, and the silken locks fell down over one eye. Turning his head into the wind, he flared his wide nostrils as he breathed in all the scents of home.

The young redheaded man at his side slipped a halter lightly over the horse's small pointed ears. The regal colt whuffled softly as familiar hands fixed the halter loosely around his head.

"What is it, boy?" Alec Ramsay soothed, giving

1

the colt a caress on the neck. "Is there something out there?"

Raven tossed his head with a sniff. Danielle had seen him do that often.

"Easy, Raven. That's a good boy."

Clipping a longe line to the halter, Alec led the colt to mid-pasture. A moment later, the colt was jogging around him in a wide circle. "Hiya! Come on, boy," Alec encouraged him. "Atta boy-ee."

The sound of Raven's hoofbeats drifted through the upper pasture, where Danielle was sitting in the grass with her best friend, Julie Burke.

"Raven sure looks like he's grown some," Julie said. "He's much bigger than the last time I saw him."

"He should be," Danielle said. "He's almost six months old now." Her eyes followed the tiny figure of the colt as he pranced in circles, first one way, then the other, in the field below. Julie smiled and turned her attention back to the *Teen Spree* magazine she was reading.

Danielle stood up and shielded her eyes with one hand. Julie was right. Raven was becoming more powerful and graceful every day. The colt weighed more than five hundred pounds and stood thirteen hands high, with a large frame and a wide, strong back. He was also at a very tricky stage of his training, just being introduced to bit, and bridle.

Alec Ramsay was doing his best to make Raven comfortable with both, but it wasn't always so easy.

Danielle took a deep breath of fresh, cool air. It was chilly today, for Florida. But it was a great day. To celebrate the beginning of winter recess from school, she had taken the morning off, borrowed a horse, and gone riding with Julie. It was something they hadn't done together for ages, not since her horse Redman had been sent away.

"I wonder what Reddy's doing right now," Danielle said.

Julie yawned. "Knowing that lazy ol' guy, he's probably off sleeping somewhere."

"He is *not* lazy," Danielle snapped defensively.

"I'm just kidding, Danielle," Julie said. "Don't be so touchy."

Danielle sighed. "I just worry about Redman sometimes."

"I know," Julie said. She waved her hand at the fields around them. "But this isn't so bad, is it?"

No, Danielle thought, *this really isn't so bad at all.*

After months of being horseless with Redman gone, it was wonderful to go riding again and explore the trails and paths crisscrossing the back woods and cow pastures surrounding Wishing Wells. Gypsy was an easy ride, Danielle thought, almost like sitting in an armchair. Gypsy was a roly-poly Arabian mare belonging to Julie's aunt Trix. She sometimes reminded Danielle of Redman. Danielle missed him so much.

It seemed like forever since he'd been shipped off to Mr. Sweet's riding camp up north. She was saving all the money she could to buy Redman and bring him home again, but she was still far from reaching her goal. If Alec Ramsay hadn't given her a break by letting her help him work with Raven, her whole plan would have been hopeless. Sometimes she thought Alec was the only one who *really* understood how she felt about her horse.

Danielle and Julie had finished eating the cheese-and-tomato sandwiches they'd brought along with them. It was nice just hanging out in the shade of the giant oak tree on the land above the Conners farmhouse.

But Danielle was beginning to get tired of sitting there with nothing to do. The article that Julie was reading aloud from *Teen Spree* was really pretty boring. *Who cares what some pop star eats for breakfast?* Danielle thought. She didn't want to hurt Julie's feelings, though. She kept that opinion to herself.

She rolled over onto her back and stared up at the clouds. The warm sun was making her feel kind of lazy. She considered getting up to pick the pretty purple flowers growing over by a broken-down fence post. The wildflowers might look great braided into Gypsy's mane. *Nah*, Danielle told herself. *Too much trouble.* She picked a piece of grass, stuck it in the corner of her mouth, and chewed thoughtfully.

"Hey, are you asleep, Danielle?" Julie asked a few moments later.

Danielle suddenly realized that her friend had stopped reading aloud. She hadn't been paying attention.

"No...well, yeah," Danielle sighed. "Sort of."

Julie put down her magazine. "So what are we going to do now that school's out?"

Danielle shrugged. "I don't know. Hang out at the farm, I guess. I'm probably going to be helping Alec with Raven. I hope so, anyway."

"Teri's going down to Key West with her dad," Julie said. "Not bad, huh?"

"Sounds nice," Danielle agreed. "I'll be lucky just to see my dad this Christmas. He's still on tour with his band."

"Don't worry," Julie said. "I'm sure he'll make it home."

"Well, I know he'll try, anyway," Danielle said. She looked back over at Gypsy. The mare was grazing peacefully next to Julie's horse, Calamity. She smiled as she remembered how her older brother, Dylan, had bumped and bounced along on Gypsy the last time they had all gone riding together. At least he had managed to hang on, Danielle told herself. Her brother wasn't much of a rider. Gypsy had to be one of the sweetest, most laid-back horses in all of Wishing Wells. It was nice of Julie's aunt to let Danielle borrow her for the afternoon like this.

Danielle and Julie gathered a couple of handfuls of blossoms and began braiding them into the horses' manes. But Danielle still felt restless.

"You want to head back?" she asked after a while, spitting out the stalk of grass she was still chewing on.

Julie sighed. "Yeah, I guess we should. This was fun, though, just doing nothing. It's a nice way to start a vacation."

Back at the farm after taking Gypsy home, Danielle ran straight to the barn to see Raven. Alec was sitting on a tack trunk outside Raven's stall, talking on his cell phone. He didn't look happy.

Danielle waved to Alec, who gave her a preoccupied nod as she headed to find Raven. The colt seemed to be taking a nap in the back of his stall.

Danielle looked over her shoulder at Alec. The trainer grinned as he held the phone away from his ear and rolled his eyes. Even from a distance, Danielle could hear the agitated man's voice on the other end. Alec got up and walked toward the tack room, putting the phone back to his ear and listening a few seconds more.

"So what am I supposed to do now?" Alec said, then listened again. "I know," Danielle heard him say with a sigh. "Right."

What is going on? Danielle wondered.

Alec listened some more. "Fine. Okay. Sure. We'll find someone. Right. See you. 'Bye."

He touched a button and slipped the phone into his jacket pocket. Then he walked into the tack room and came back a moment later with a jumbo-sized bottle of Tums. He snapped the lid off and gobbled a couple of tablets, crunching them with his teeth.

"So was that bad news on the phone or something?" Danielle asked.

"Oh, we have a little trouble with a van coming down," Alec said casually. "Nothing important. One groom isn't working for us all of a sudden, another is home sick. I was counting on both of them to help me bring some horses down south."

"Can't you get someone else?" Danielle asked.

"Sure," Alec said, running a hand through his red hair. He looked worried. "We'd better, anyway. And soon. Those horses have to be here in Florida in four days."

"Gosh, I wish I could go." The words rose to Danielle's lips and were out before she even knew that she'd said them.

"I wish you could, too," Alec said.

His response caught Danielle by surprise. Was Alec serious?

"You mean it?" she asked cautiously.

Alec nodded. "Sure. The job's not too hard. Someone just has to ride in the back of the van with the horses and keep them company during the trip. Maybe you could ask your brother, too, if he's in the market for some extra money. I really could use both of you. And the job is a snap."

Danielle thought for a moment. "Well," she said slowly, "we're not in school right now. Vacation started yesterday."

Alec nodded. "Yeah, I know. I saw you up in the pasture today."

Danielle glanced toward Raven's stall. "But what about our Little Buddy?"

"I can move him over to South Wind for a few days," Alec said. "He needs looking after right now, and it'll be easier for Billy to keep an eye on him there. Henry Dailey said he might be coming down, too."

Danielle had never met the trainer of Alec's famous horse, the Black. She'd heard about him, though, and about his reputation as a tough, no-nonsense trainer who brought home winners for his owners. It would be Henry's first visit to see how Alec was getting along with the Hopeful Farm racehorses in Florida this winter.

"So the offer stands," Alec continued. "You're a good groom, and like I said, I'm sure you could handle the job. Let me know by tonight, okay? You and Dylan, if he's interested, would have to be ready to go tomorrow night."

"I'll ask him and my mom about it right away," Danielle promised. A trip up north and back with a whole bunch of horses and a chance to earn some money, too? This was an opportunity she couldn't pass up.

Her mom just *had* to say yes!

➳ CHAPTER TWO ᐸᑊ

The Bizzles

"No way, no day," Mrs. Conners said crossly, tossing down her briefcase and dropping into one of the over-stuffed porch chairs. She had just returned home from work and she looked really tired. Danielle hadn't even waited for her mom to get in the house before explaining about Alec's job offer. *Bad move,* Danielle told herself.

"But Mom," she pleaded, talking fast and thinking faster. "Alec will be there the whole time, and Dylan wants to go, too. Dad says it's okay with him. I mean, if it's okay with you."

Mrs. Conners gave her a stern look. "You're telling me you've already called your father about this?"

Danielle nodded. "Just before you got here."

"I bet," Mrs. Conners said, furrowing her eyebrows. "Do you know how much all these phone calls are costing us, young lady?"

"I know, Mom," Danielle said, then added quickly, "But Dad said Dylan and I might even be able to meet up with him and the band somewhere along the way, if we can plan it out with Alec."

A serious quiet hung in the air. *Maybe she's starting to crack,* Danielle thought.

"Bring me the phone," Mrs. Conners said finally. "We'll *discuss* it. I have to talk to your father about something else anyway."

"All right!" Danielle said, hopping off to get the telephone.

"You've hardly ever been outside of Wishing Wells," Mrs. Conners said, shaking her head as Danielle handed her the phone. "Now you want to go to New York City."

Danielle gave her mom a hug. "You're the greatest, Mom."

"I said we'll *discuss* it, Danielle," Mom said patiently. "As in, talk about it. Nobody's going anywhere just yet."

"Okay, okay," Danielle said eagerly. *I can't believe this,* Danielle thought. *She's giving in!* With a sigh, Mrs. Conners started punching in the phone number.

By the next night, Danielle was a nervous wreck. She was trying to relax, but nothing seemed to work. She stood up, walked over to the TV, and switched it off. She couldn't even concentrate on her favorite program.

Her bags were packed, and she was ready to go. In a couple of hours, she, Dylan, and Alec Ramsay would be on an airplane headed north, where they would pick up a vanload of racehorses. Then they would drive them home to Florida. She still couldn't believe that her mother had actually agreed to let her brother and her go off on this trip, even with Alec along to keep an eye out. But it was true. The trainer was due to pick them up in forty-five minutes.

She was so eager to get started on this adventure that she could hardly stand it. If she wasn't careful, she might come down with a severe case of the Bizzles.

Danielle jerked to a stop, right in the middle of the family room. *Where in the world did I get that word?* she wondered. A television commercial? She had no idea why the word "Bizzles" had entered her mind. It sounded like a brand of laundry soap. She could almost hear some cheerful housewife announcing, "Give your clothes that bubbly Bizzle feeling." Obviously, sitting around and waiting like this was driving her nuts.

Just then, she remembered something her mother had taught her once. It was a yoga exercise that was supposed to help when you couldn't get to sleep at night. Maybe the exercise could help her get through this attack of the Bizzles.

The exercise was called the Corpse, or something creepy like that.

Danielle flopped down on her back. She closed her eyes and took a deep breath. She tried to think of calm, peaceful things: snowcapped mountains on a faraway horizon, a calm ocean, a forest at twilight. *Bizzles be gone,* Danielle chanted silently.

After a few minutes, Danielle gave up. It was a dumb idea, anyway.

She jumped to her feet and went over to the window, gazing out into the darkness.

Less than an hour to go.

For about the tenth time, Danielle walked out to the barn, just for something to do. She was about to check up on Raven, the barn's only current resident, until she remembered that his stall was empty. The colt was already over at South Wind for an early-morning appointment to see the vet.

Back in the house, she found her brother in the kitchen. He was searching through drawers, looking for batteries. Dylan was fourteen, two years older than Danielle. Like Danielle, he had reddish blond hair, and his cheeks were lightly spotted with freckles. People sometimes mistook them for twins.

"Are you ready, Dylan?" Danielle asked.

Dylan frowned, peering into another drawer. "I'll be ready in five minutes," he said.

Somehow, Danielle doubted that. Her brother

always put things off till the last minute.

"Yeah, sure," she said.

"I will." Dylan was starting on the cabinets now.

"Come on, Dylan," Danielle said, following her brother around the kitchen. "Alec's going to be here soon."

"Quit bugging me, D," Dylan snapped. "He's not due for another hour."

"It's only half an hour now. You'd better be ready."

"Shut up, or I'm not going."

Danielle quickly closed her mouth.

Dylan ran upstairs and came back down a few minutes later with a knapsack. "I can't believe that Mom really went for this crazy idea of yours," he said.

"I think it helped that we're going to be working together," Danielle said.

"Hey, it'll be worth it if there's a chance we can really meet up with Dad. That's the only reason Mom agreed, I'm sure."

Dylan began to make himself a peanut butter sandwich. Danielle shook her head as she watched him add an extra layer of bread. Her brother was always eating.

She walked outside and sat down in the wooden rocker on the porch. A few minutes later, Dylan joined her. Danielle leaned forward and rested her chin on the railing, her eyes straining into the distance. A pair of headlight beams shone off in the distance; something was approaching along the county road that ran by her family's farm. She watched expectantly as the lights came closer.

"Nope," Dylan said. He sounded as disappointed as Danielle felt. "Too big." The lights drew closer and proved to belong to a giant moving van. The van continued past the entrance to the driveway and barreled off through the night.

"False alarm," Danielle said with a sigh. She drummed her fingers on the arm of her chair. Noticing that they were wet with perspiration, she wiped them quickly on her pant legs. "It's nearly ten," she said, glancing at her watch. "Alec should be here any minute now."

She turned her attention back to the highway, watching for headlights, listening for the far-off drone of a car engine. Waiting. Waiting. Bizzling.

Beside her, Dylan rocked back and forth in the rocking chair under the porch lamp. He was reading a road map of the East Coast. Danielle quit staring out into the empty night and looked over his shoulder.

"I guess we'll just book it straight down I-95," Dylan said.

Danielle followed his finger as he traced their route south. "New York to Baltimore to Washington to Richmond." He named places that Danielle had heard about but never seen. "Then to Rocky Mount to Columbia to..."

"Rocky Mount!" Danielle exclaimed, interrupting her brother. "That's where Mr. Sweet's riding camp is. That's where Redman is!"

"So?"

"I wonder...Maybe we could stop by and say hi to Redman, too."

"Right." Dylan chuckled. "I'm sure we're gonna visit your dumb old horse."

"Why not?" Danielle asked indignantly.

"Because," her brother sneered, "this isn't some pleasure tour of the East Coast we're going on, you know. This is a job. We probably won't even get to see Dad."

Danielle thought there was a good chance she might get to see Redman. More than anyone, Alec knew how she felt about her horse. In fact, he understood practically better than anyone else. It would be asking a lot, she knew. Still...

"Alec might go for it," she said.

Dylan shook his head doubtfully. "Face it, squirt. Once we get up north, all that's going to happen is that we're going to get stuck in the back of a horse van for the next couple of days. There might not even be a window to look out of. We'll probably end up staring at a bunch of horses the whole trip."

Danielle shrugged. "Sounds okay to me."

"Yeah, to you it probably would."

Danielle dropped the subject and leaned over the railing to watch for cars again. "So you don't really want to go?"

"I didn't say that," Dylan said. "Hey, anything to get out of here for a while."

Dylan was having troubles with his girlfriend, Nicole, Danielle knew. She wasn't sure, but she had a feeling her brother had been dumped.

"Did you see the note Mom left for us in the kitchen?" Dylan asked.

"Yeah. We're supposed to call every day, I know."

Their mom, a graphic designer, was working on a freelance project in Orlando and had said good-bye to them that morning. Danielle was a little surprised her mom had been so cool about this whole thing, and now she was missing the big send-off.

Suddenly a lone pair of headlights streaked down the road. A few moments later, a familiar pickup truck wheeled into the Conners' driveway.

Alec tapped a quick beep on the horn and pulled to a stop.

Danielle ran back into the house for her knapsack. Dylan was right behind her.

Alec left the motor running and jumped out of the truck. He jogged up the porch steps. "Hey, sorry I'm late. Are you two ready?" he called through the screen door.

"Ready," they answered together.

"Okay, let's go."

Danielle and Dylan threw their knapsacks into the back of the truck and climbed in the passenger-side door.

Alec gave them both a quick glance and nodded approvingly at their fiber-filled windbreakers. "Those jackets will come in handy. It could be cold up north." Then he shifted the truck into gear, and they were on their way to the airport.

Danielle could see that Alec was full of energy and looking forward to the trip. He was grinning from ear to ear. "Noo Yawk Citay, here we come," he said, playing up his Yankee accent.

Danielle settled back against the seat. Finally, their big adventure was beginning!

CHAPTER THREE

A Shaky Welcome

"Well, folks," came the friendly voice of the pilot over the main cabin speaker system, "we have been cleared for approach and will be landing at La Guardia Airport in about fifteen minutes. New York is clear and cold. The temperature is twenty-five degrees. Fasten your seat belts, please. Sorry about the little delay."

Danielle already had her seat belt on. She'd had it on practically the whole plane trip, except for the one time when she'd gone to the bathroom. She wasn't used to flying, and it had been a pretty bumpy ride.

They'd been in a holding pattern over the New York metro area for the past forty-five minutes. Danielle had been sitting in the window seat, her face glued to the port. This was her first trip north. She'd never seen a really big city like New York before.

Or snow.

"See any white patches down there?" Alec asked. He was next to Danielle and was craning his neck to get a look at the lights below. He seemed glad to be home in the New York City area again.

"I think so," she said. "It's kind of hard to tell in the dark."

"This will be your first time to see snow, right?" Alec said.

Danielle smiled. "Yes. I can't wait." She turned back to the window. Outside, a crescent moon shone over a sea of lights: yellow, white, big, small. Some were strung neatly like pearls, others like tangled strands of Christmas-tree lights.

"Didn't you say this is your first time up north, too?" Alec asked Dylan. Danielle's brother was sitting in the middle seat.

"Yeah, I've only been as far as Atlanta and Mobile a couple times with Dad."

Danielle looked away from the window for a second to see Alec give Dylan a wry smile. She knew Alec was fiercely proud of coming from New York. He'd once told her that there was no place like it anywhere in the country—even in the world. During the flight, Alec had been listening to some of the other passengers speaking. Just from their accents and the way they said certain words, he could tell where they were from: New Jersey, Long Island, or the Bronx. It seemed to be a kind of game for him.

They flew over an oil refinery, its smokestacks spitting fire like birthday candles on a cake. Danielle elbowed her brother. "Hey, Dylan, check this out."

Her brother peeked over her shoulder. "Where?"

"Down there!" Danielle said, annoyed. Dylan could act really dumb sometimes.

"There's too much reflection in the window," he said, shrugging. "I can't see a thing." Then he sat back in his seat and returned to acting cool.

Danielle kept staring out the window as the plane swept through the night. Soon she felt the plane start dropping lower and lower, and her ears began to pop. On one last turn over the city, the entire cabin tilted up so that all three of them could see the spectacular view. As they continued to fly low over the city, Alec pointed out different landmarks. "There's the Empire State Building and the Chrysler Building. Hey, look, the twin towers of the World Trade Center, and the Brooklyn Bridge." Dylan gave up his Mr. Cool act and peered out the window like everyone else.

"I wish we had time to go into the city a bit," Alec said. "You two would really like it. Maybe some other time when we're not on such a tight schedule."

"Where did you say we were spending the night?" Dylan asked.

"Tonight we're going out to a place in Queens,

near Aqueduct Racetrack," Alec replied. "There's a little motel there that gives discounts to horsemen. Henry reserved us a couple of rooms. We'll pick up the horses in the morning."

As the plane dropped farther, Danielle saw more traces of gray-white snow on the ground. A sudden high-pitched whine and a harsh clanking sound made her grip the seat rests beside her tightly. "It's okay," Alec assured her. "It's just the plane's landing gear unfolding and locking into position." Danielle nodded, gulping, as the plane skimmed over buildings and highways. When she dared to look again, she could see cars and everything else on the ground very clearly.

They landed with a bump, taxied down a long runway, and after what seemed to be forever to Danielle, arrived at their gate. As the plane came to a full stop and everyone began unbuckling their seat belts, Danielle was glad that Alec had insisted they pack light and bring just their overnight stuff. That way, they didn't need to go to the baggage claim.

"Here we go, guys," Alec said. "Stay with me, okay?" Taking the lead, he strode quickly through the airport, Danielle and Dylan close at his heels. The airport was crowded, with travelers rushing about, many of them carrying bags full of holiday gifts. Danielle had never seen so many people in her life.

Reaching the metal detectors by the main lobby, Alec spotted a man waiting there and waved. The man was a tough, leathery-looking guy in a well-worn felt fedora, the kind Danielle had seen people wear sometimes in old movies. *That has to be Henry Dailey,* Danielle thought.

Alec walked up to the man, who shook hands warmly with him, then tilted his head curiously at Dylan and Danielle, who were standing to one side. Danielle thought she saw a flash of surprise in his penetrating blue eyes.

After a moment, Alec introduced them with a casual wave in their direction. "Henry, this is Danielle and Dylan Conners. They're the grooms I told you about."

Henry automatically shook hands with Danielle and her brother. His hand felt big and callused. He started to say something to Alec, then stopped.

"Excuse us a moment, will you, kids?" he said, his voice polite but firm. He walked a few steps away and stood, rocking back and forth on his heels. "Come here a second, Alec."

When Alec went over, Henry put his arm around him and turned so their backs were to Danielle and Dylan. Then he started talking in a low voice. Feeling awkward, Danielle looked away to watch the other travelers passing by.

It was plain to see that Henry Dailey was concerned about her and Dylan. Henry wasn't ranting or anything, but Danielle could still catch a few words.

"You didn't...Who *are* these kids?...*Grooms?*...We should trust *kids* with some of our best horses?"

"I know they're a little young, Henry," Alec began.

The trainer looked back at Danielle and her brother and frowned. "Yeah. You can say that again."

Alec's voice took on a slight edge. "Come on, Henry. If you hadn't fired Tommy..."

"We can do better, and you know it," Henry hissed.

"I'm telling you, these kids can do the job," Alec insisted. "You said yourself it shouldn't be too tough. Trust me, will you, Henry?"

"Who's taking care of the colt, then? Billy? Just one guy? That's a valuable animal."

Danielle and Dylan exchanged glances. Alec was talking fast now. "Give me a break, Henry. Raven's fine. These are smart kids. They know what's what. It's not like we have a lot of choice."

"Fine," Henry said gravely, giving up. "Just remember, *you're* responsible."

Alec turned back to Danielle and Dylan. The looks on their faces must have made it plain that they had overheard some of what Alec and Henry had been talking about. Alec smiled at them and calmly held up one hand. "Everything's okay," he said. "Let's go."

Henry went striding ahead through the terminal with Alec at his heels. The two were in deep conversation about conditions at Hopeful Farm. The man in the battered fedora walked with a funny swaying motion that Alec unconsciously began imitating as he caught up and walked along beside him.

"This is pretty exciting, huh?" Danielle said to her brother.

"Yeah," Dylan said. "Looks like we surprised Mr. Dailey, though."

The cold air outside the airport didn't feel too bad, Danielle thought, not too much different from some chilly nights at home. *Well,* she told herself, zipping up her jacket, *maybe a little colder. In fact, it's freezing.*

They all piled into a cab, with Henry in front and Alec, Dylan, and Danielle in back. Soon they were speeding through the dark December night toward Aqueduct Racetrack. The highway was busy even at this late hour, and everyone seemed to be driving really fast. Danielle held on to the strap next to her head for dear life.

Alec and Henry didn't say much to each other in the taxi. Danielle couldn't tell if Henry was really mad or whether he just always looked that way. She was startled when the trainer suddenly turned to look at her over his shoulder and casually started talking to her about Raven.

"Alec tells me you've done a real fine job helping with the colt," Henry said lightly.

"Thank you, sir," Danielle said in her best grown-up voice. "It seems like he's getting bigger and stronger every day."

"So I hear," Henry said, nodding. "I guess I'll see for myself soon enough. After we get the horses in the van squared away and on the road tomorrow, I'm going to be flying down to Florida myself."

"You are?" Danielle said. She wasn't sure whether that was a good thing or not. "I mean, great."

Henry nodded toward Alec. "I think it's about time I came down to see what my pal Alec's been doing with Hopeful Farm's money this past month or so."

"Don't worry so much, will you, Henry?" Alec said, looking out the window.

What is Henry so worried about? Danielle wondered. *Is it Raven, or Dylan and me taking care of such valuable horses?*

Or something else?

CHAPTER FOUR

Snowballs

The taxi finally sped off the highway and into the Marquis Motel Inn's parking lot. Danielle stepped out of the cab. She was really starting to feel the difference in the weather now. It was like walking into a refrigerator. Henry paid the driver and then showed Danielle and Dylan to their room. He and Alec were right next door.

Dropping her bag on a chair, Danielle claimed one of the beds and started jumping around on it. "You're going to break the bed, Danielle," her brother scolded her. "Grow up, will you?"

Danielle bounced a few more times and then jumped off the bed to the floor. "This is great! I've never stayed in a motel room without Mom or Dad before. Now we can do whatever we want!"

"Shhh!" Dylan said. "Be quiet, will you? You're going to wake someone up and get us kicked out of here."

"Chill, Dylan," Danielle said. "I'm not hurting anything." She picked up a pillow and threw it across the room at her brother. Dylan dodged the pillow.

"Right. Just remember who Mom put in charge of this little expedition. The chain of command goes Alec, me, and then you."

Danielle put on her most angelic smile. "Sure, Dylan. Whatever you say."

Dylan glared at her. "Don't get cute, D. I'm going to see if Alec wants us to do anything tonight or if we should just go to sleep or what. You stay here."

"Okay, Mr. Big Boss with the Red Hot sauce."

Dylan sidestepped, ducking another flying pillow, and walked outside.

Danielle sat on the edge of the bed listening as her brother knocked on Alec's door and went inside. Dylan knew about a tenth as much as she did about horses. Being bossed around by Henry and Alec was one thing, but she wasn't about to take orders from her dumb brother. She'd show Mr. Cool.

Stepping outside the motel room, she found a patch of fairly clean snow. Taking a handful of cold, wet white stuff, she packed it into a snowball. She marveled at her icy creation a moment, as her bare hands began to tingle and practically go numb. This was her very first snowball!

She could hear Alec talking to Dylan, and her

She could hear Alec talking to Dylan, and her brother's muffled reply. Then the motel-room door opened, and Dylan stepped out.

"Get some sleep," Alec called after him. "We'll be up before dawn."

"Okay, good night, then," Dylan said, closing the door.

Danielle took careful aim and fired the snowball at her brother.

At the same time, the door to Alec's room swung open, and Henry Dailey stepped through the doorway in his pajamas, carrying an ice bucket in his hands. The snowball missed Dylan by a foot, sailing past him and splattering on the wall right beside Henry's head.

Danielle gasped. "Oops, s-sorry," she stammered.

Dylan looked at her as if she was out of her mind.

Henry just glanced over at Danielle, completely unfazed, and shook his head. Then he continued on toward the ice machine at the end of the building.

Danielle sheepishly slipped back into her and Dylan's hotel room and closed the door. Her brother followed a moment later. She braced herself for him to start yelling.

"Good job, Danielle," Dylan said. "You nearly whacked Henry Dailey on the head." Then his face broke out in a huge grin. Soon they were both

"I can't believe he didn't say anything," Danielle said finally.

"I know," Dylan said. "You were pretty lucky."

Danielle went into the bathroom and rummaged around in her toiletries bag for her toothbrush. "Alec told me about Henry once," she said. "He says that under that rough exterior beats the heart of a real softy."

"Maybe so," Dylan said. "But you heard Henry. He thinks we're too young for this job as it is. I don't think throwing a snowball at him helped matters much."

Now Danielle felt terribly guilty. She really wanted to prove herself trustworthy on this job. Now she'd almost blown the whole thing. And all because of that stupid snowball.

"We have to call Mom," Dylan said suddenly. He started patting his pockets. "Where is that calling card Mom gave me before we left?"

"On the table next to the phone," Danielle called, drying her face with a towel. At least she was good for *something*.

After they'd called their mom in Orlando, Danielle climbed into bed. She worried awhile as she lay awake. Had she really blown things with Henry Dailey? Would he fire them before they even started the job? On the other hand, it sounded as if Henry and Alec were having trouble finding grooms. Maybe Henry was stuck with the two of them, like it or not. She tossed and turned a few minutes more and finally fell fast asleep.

It was still pitch-black outside when Alec pounded on the door of their room just after five the next morning.

"Up and at 'em, you two sleepyheads," he called. "Time's a-wastin'."

Danielle rolled over in bed and rubbed her eyes. "Okay," she called back. "We're awake."

"We'll meet you in the lobby in fifteen minutes," Alec said. "And hey, leave the snow outside, okay?"

"Good going, Danielle." Dylan looked up from his pillow and shook his head.

"He was kidding, Dylan," Danielle said. She hoped.

Dylan suddenly jumped out of bed and sprinted for the shower. Danielle made a mad rush to beat him to it.

"Shower first," she announced as they both grabbed for the bathroom doorknob at the same time.

"Come on, D," Dylan said.

Danielle shook her head. "No go, bro. Ladies first."

Dylan groaned. "If I have to wait for you, we'll be here all morning."

Danielle showered and dressed quickly, then

turned the bathroom over to her brother. "See?" she said as he elbowed past her and slammed the bathroom door. "I was in there less than three minutes." She stuffed her toiletries bag into her knapsack and zipped it closed. "I'm going to the lobby to find Alec," Danielle called to Dylan through the bathroom door.

The crisp early-morning air filled her lungs as she stepped outside. After a night in the stuffy motel room, it felt sort of good. Or maybe she was just getting used to the cold. She zipped her jacket up tight and walked quickly toward the lobby.

Off by itself at the far end of the parking lot, Danielle saw a big green and yellow horse van parked under a street lamp. A string of red lights ran along the van's high roof, and the words "Hopeful Farm" were printed on the side.

Wow, Danielle thought. She could just see them zooming down the highway in that! If she and Dylan got a chance to see their dad, he would certainly be impressed. The van was much bigger than the bus he and his whole band traveled in when they were on tour.

Not bad, she thought. *We're traveling in style.*

This was going to be great.

CHAPTER FIVE

"The Big A"

When Danielle walked into the lobby, Alec was already there, reading a newspaper. There were complimentary doughnuts and coffee on a table beside the registration desk.

"'Morning, Danielle." Alec pointed to another table at the far end of the lobby. "There's milk and some little boxes of cereal over there, if you want. You'd better get something to eat now. Once we get rolling, who knows when we'll be stopping again."

Danielle was on her second bowl of cornflakes by the time Dylan showed up. He found the food all on his own and began wolfing down doughnuts. When Danielle had finished her breakfast, she moved over next to Alec.

"I saw the van in the parking lot," she said. "Pretty awesome. How many horses can you fit in something like that?"

"A lot." Alec smiled. "More than we could handle, probably. But don't worry. We're traveling light this time. Quality, not quantity, this trip."

Just then Henry came to the lobby door and beckoned. Alec looked at his watch. "Okay, guys. Let's get moving."

Danielle and Dylan followed Henry to the van. It was an enormous eighteen-wheeler with oval-shaped tinted windows. Danielle thought it looked like some sort of weird giant insect. As they crossed the parking lot, an icy breeze swept over them. Danielle pulled her jacket close around her.

Alec waved Danielle and Dylan to the front of the van. "You guys can sit next to me in the front seat," he said. "There's plenty of room. And you'll get to see more of where we are from here than you would in back."

Henry jumped into the driver's seat, with Alec in the middle and Dylan and Danielle sharing the window seat. Danielle ended up sitting on her brother's lap because there wasn't as much room in front as Alec thought. "Man, are *you* heavy," Dylan complained.

Danielle just glared at him.

They drove out onto the street and through a neighborhood of tightly packed houses. The van's headlights dipped in front of them as the engine's noise rose and fell with the shifting of gears.

Alec turned the heater on, but the cold still

seeped in around the doors and windows of the van. Danielle shivered and thought of how warm it was back home in Florida.

Turning a tight corner, the van almost sideswiped an early-morning jogger. The man jumped out of the way, slamming up against a brick wall to keep from getting clipped by the van. Everyone looked at Henry, who was frowning behind the wheel.

"Oops," Alec said.

"I'm getting too old for this," Henry complained, cranking the steering wheel left.

At the gate of the Aqueduct Racetrack, Henry slowed the van to a crawl, and the guard waved them through. Beyond the rows of barns, Danielle could see the edge of the oval-shaped track and the stadium-sized grandstands. "Wow," she said. "I never thought it would be so big." So far, everything in New York was big.

Henry edged the van forward until they came to the loading area of the receiving barn. "Here we are," Alec announced. "Welcome to Aqueduct, the Big A."

As they all got out of the van, Alec touched Danielle on the shoulder. "Let me show you and Dylan to your seats in back. That's where you'll be stationed once we get going with the horses."

The two of them followed Alec around to the

side of the van, stepping to a door behind the driver's seat. For Danielle, it was a bit of a jump to the first step, but luckily there was a handle to grab on to just outside the door. Dylan climbed up behind her and Alec.

Alec flipped the lights on inside. The compartment was small, basically a short aisle with two benches. It was separated by a partition from the front part of the van. There was an Arbuckle Feed Store calendar with a picture of a horse on it on the wall. Another compartment held tack and tools, another sawdust, another hay. Behind that were the stalls.

Alec waved toward the benches. "They're big enough to sleep on if you scrunch up a bit. Feel free to take a nap, as long as one of you is awake to keep an eye on the horses."

"Oh, we'll both stay awake, don't worry," Dylan assured him quickly.

Alec smiled. "Whatever. Listen, I'm going to start getting the horses. You guys wait here a second until I get things organized. Maybe you can help. We'll see, okay?"

Danielle and Dylan both nodded.

"I feel like we're supposed to be hiding in here," Dylan said after Alec left.

Danielle shrugged. "Maybe. Henry probably doesn't want to be reminded we're around."

"Hey, who cares?" Dylan said. "Baby-sitting a bunch of horses can't be too bad. At least I don't have to be cleaning up some barn."

Danielle nodded, barely paying attention. She was thinking about Aqueduct. *How many great racehorses must have walked around back here?* she wondered. *This is one of the most famous racetracks in the world.*

A minute later, the back doors of the van swung open. It was Henry. "Okay, you two. You might as well come out here till we get these horses loaded up."

Danielle jumped down and walked around to the back of the van, where Henry was settling the ramp in place. Behind him, in single file, stood five of the most beautiful horses Danielle had ever seen.

CHAPTER SIX

Trouble

Alec stood at the head of the lead horse, a tall, light golden chestnut with four white stockings. A prominent white blaze was splashed from between her eyes to the tip of her nose.

Behind the mare were two red bays, slim and elegant. Then came a showy gray who held her head proudly.

The last horse was perhaps the most beautiful of all, a speedy-looking black filly with a high-arched neck. Now Danielle could really see what Alec meant when he'd said they would be carrying quality on this trip.

Behind Alec, at the head of each horse, stood a group of handlers: two older men in overalls, a stocky blond girl, and a long-haired younger man. Alec led the chestnut mare. She stopped and began pawing the ground, then she threw her head in the air. "Easy, pretty mama," Alec soothed. The mare danced briefly at the end of the lead shank.

All of the horses were blanketed with stable sheets, and their legs were wrapped in shipping bandages. A small crowd of horse people stood admiring the horses from a respectful distance.

The jittery mare kept her head up and her ears started flickering in all directions at once. "I saw that coming," someone said as the mare half-reared. "He needs to walk those horses around the barn a few times."

"Ramsey knows what he's doing," someone snapped.

"Shhh," hissed the two older grooms.

Looking annoyed, Alec unzipped his jacket and pulled off his sweatshirt and wrapped it around the mare's head. Taking a firm hold of her lead, he clucked softly to her. Finally, the horse gave a bored-sounding sigh, tapped the ramp with one hoof, then walked meekly into the van. There was a quick rush of hoofbeats as the rest of the horses followed her up the ramp.

Danielle noticed two men standing slightly off to one side of the small crowd. They were talking together intently as they watched the horses load.

One of the men, wearing a long trench coat, looked familiar. Danielle wondered if he was Luke Stedman, the trainer of Brandlin, one of the big three-year-old racehorses the year before. *Look at that suntan,* she thought. *It probably* is *him.* Danielle knew Stedman was based in Ocala, Florida, not far from where she lived, in Wishing Wells. She moved a little closer to try to hear what the two men were saying.

"That two-year-old gray looks nice," said the man in the baseball cap beside Stedman.

Stedman nodded. "She has stride, and she has mind."

"A lot of horses can be frantic. You want to put a glass bubble around them so they can't hurt themselves. That one is so laid-back. She's like a stable pony. And she has that long stride, just travels over ground."

Stedman frowned. "Henry had a good reason to buy her."

The guy in the cap scratched his chin thoughtfully. "When you spend a hundred grand of someone else's money, you'd better have a good reason. I hear he bought her for some retired stockbroker from Miami who—"

"Danielle! Dylan!" Alec called from inside the van. "Come in here, will you?"

Danielle quit eavesdropping and ran back to the van. She quickly climbed through the door behind Dylan, and they headed back to the stalls, where Alec was waiting for them.

Alec gestured to the tall chestnut filly. "I want

you guys to meet the guests you are going to be traveling with. This is Maradona. She is a native of Argentina, like Prima." Danielle nodded, remembering Raven's dam, who had been stabled at her family's farm until a month or so ago.

"The bay in the next stall is Evernite," Alec said. "She's always good about traveling. See, she's settled right down inside the stall. But when she comes on the track, she usually prances, like a fighter shadowboxing in the ring." Alec moved to another horse. "This is her little sister, Severlite. They're both Florida-breds. Going home, just like you knuckleheads," Alec added with a grin.

He moved over to the gray. Her coat was the color of a cloud during a tropical summer storm. "Ninadja here has a placid manner around the barn, but don't let her good looks fool you. When the gates open, she's all business. Like Evernite, Ninadja is pretty laid-back. You could shoot a cannon off beside her and she wouldn't flinch."

Alec moved to the back. "Darsky is the cannon," he went on, indicating the beautiful black filly. "She was sired by the Black. High-strung. You never know if she'll explode before a race. But she's gotten better in the last year. She has the same running style as the Black—stays off the pace and then makes her move in the homestretch."

The filly tossed her head, snorting and pawing at

the wood shavings on the floor. Then she stopped fussing and pulled a mouthful of hay from the mesh-rope sling in front of her.

Alec looked at Dylan and Danielle. "Watch her now. If anyone causes trouble on this trip, chances are it'll be Darsky."

A few minutes later, as Danielle was bringing Alec a cup of coffee from inside the barn, she saw Henry step out of the van. Luke Stedman came around the corner and pulled Henry off to the side as Danielle passed by.

"Say, Henry, I wanted to ask you something," she heard the silver-haired man in the trench coat say. "All my vans are in use right now. Would it be okay if I put a horse in with yours going down?"

Henry thought about this for a moment, then shrugged. "I guess we're going to the same place."

"I'd appreciate it."

"Sure," Henry agreed. "If it'd help you out, go ahead."

Danielle walked over to Alec and handed him his coffee. Alec was double-checking the van and getting it ready, testing the hooks where the horses were tied up. Luke Stedman poked his head in through the van door a few moments later.

"You got yourself another horse going back," he told Alec, handing him a slip of paper.

Alec looked at the slip of paper and shook his

head. "No way, not unless you clear it with Henry."

"Henry says it's okay to put him in."

Alec seemed a little surprised but nodded. "Okay, if Henry says so."

Soon the horses were set to go. Danielle and Dylan were waiting for orders at the ramp when Stedman's horse appeared suddenly from around the corner, led by a nervous-looking groom.

As soon as Danielle saw the horse, she knew there was going to be trouble. The colt seemed full of himself, dropping his head down and swinging it from side to side, snorting and blowing. He moved closer to the ramp.

Henry looked up from where he was talking to a man holding a clipboard. "Hold it right there!" he hollered at the groom. In two jumps, Henry was at the colt's head. "Where do you think you're going with this here animal?"

The groom, who barely had the colt under control, shrugged helplessly. "The boss told me to bring him here and load him up."

Danielle swallowed and stepped out of the way, moving quietly to the van door. Henry looked *really* mad. She didn't want to be anywhere near him right now. She climbed into the van and peered out through the doorway.

Hearing the commotion, Luke Stedman came barging out of the barn office and headed for

Henry. "You just said I could send the horse back with you, Dailey," he said. "What's the problem here?"

"You lying son of a gun!" Henry fumed. "You never said you were sending back some stud colt to get in there with my fillies! I ought to have your license for this. Get that animal out of here and don't *ever* ask to put another horse in with mine again, you hear?"

Stedman gave Henry a bewildered look and stormed off. Henry glanced around quickly, looking for Alec, who was standing by the ramp. "Alec," Henry hollered, "get up there and get that van out of here! Right *now!*"

The poor groom was desperately trying to lead his colt under the shedrow, but now that the horse had scented the vanload of fillies, he was even wilder than before. Alec felt sorry for the groom and, in spite of Henry's orders, went to give him a hand. Together they managed to lead the colt, kicking and screaming, back to the receiving barn.

Red-faced and furious, Henry peered inside the van for a quick check. All his fillies were standing quietly in their boxes.

"They're fine," Danielle told him. She had to say something, the way Henry was looking at her.

"Don't worry, Mr. Dailey," Dylan spoke up. "We'll keep an eye on them."

Danielle couldn't believe it. All the commotion, the screaming, the unruly colt—none of it had bothered the horses in the van. It was as if they had things other than some silly colt on their minds. Or maybe they were just as anxious to get going as Danielle.

Evernite nickered at Danielle, one hoof idly pawing through the shavings.

"I know, I know," Danielle told the bay. "We're going home."

ᏊᏅ CHAPTER SEVEN ᏟᏁ

On the Road at Last

When Alec returned from helping the groom get the colt back to his stall, neither he nor Henry said a word. Alec just glanced at Henry and shrugged. Henry scowled back, but that was all. Danielle shuddered. *I sure wouldn't want Henry Dailey mad at* me *like that,* she thought. But he and Alec seemed to have some sort of understanding. Then Alec climbed into the van, waved to Henry through the windshield, and started the engine.

The big diesel hummed to life. Alec leaned out the window when Henry stepped over.

"See you in Florida," the old trainer said, all business once again. Alec nodded and cautiously eased the van forward, following the way to the gate.

Inside the van, Danielle could hear the thud of hooves as the horses moved to keep their balance.

"How's everybody doing back there?" Alec called through the partition.

"Fine," Dylan called.

"Good," said Danielle. The van passed through the racetrack's gate and turned onto the local road leading to the highway. Slowly, they picked up speed.

Leaning toward the partition, Danielle asked, "How far do you think we'll get by tonight, Alec?"

"Oh, somewhere around Rocky Mount, North Carolina, I guess."

Rocky Mount! Danielle couldn't believe her ears. They were going to be stopping in the same town as Mr. Sweet's riding camp, where her horse, Redman, was earning his oats for the time being.

"Alec, that's where Redman is, remember?" Danielle said.

There was a pause. "Oh, really?" Alec said offhandedly. There was something knowing in his tone of voice.

Danielle swallowed. "Yeah, you didn't know that?"

"Rocky Mount, huh?"

"Right near there."

There was a pause, and then Alec laughed. "I'll tell you what, Danielle," he said. "We're going to stop for gas pretty soon. You call and see where the camp is. If it's not too far off the highway, maybe we can stop by. I'd let you use my cell phone, but I forgot to charge it up and the batteries are dead."

Danielle let out a whoop and slapped her brother on the shoulder. "I'm going to see Redman!" she cried in an "I told you so" way. She knew she was driving him nuts.

"*Maybe* you're going to see him," he corrected.

"No, I will, I will, I just know I will!" Danielle practically sang.

Dylan rolled his eyes at her, then turned his attention back to the *Mad* magazine he'd brought with him.

Danielle looked up Mr. Sweet's number in the address book in her knapsack. When she found it, she did a quick drumroll with her hands on the bench beside her. "I can't believe this," she said. "I've missed Redman so much. And I just know he misses me, too."

"You'd better call your buddy Mr. Sweet before you get too excited, D," Dylan reminded her coolly without looking up from his reading.

Danielle cringed. Talking to Mr. Sweet wasn't something she really looked forward to. But no one could dampen her spirits right now, not even her know-it-all brother. What she had secretly hoped for from the beginning of this trip looked like it just might happen if only...

Stop it, Danielle scolded herself. *Dylan's right. I can't get my hopes up. There are so many ifs.*

It seemed like forever to Danielle before they

stopped for gas. So far, the horses in the back were behaving themselves, even Darsky.

Danielle ran over in her head what she wanted to say to Mr. Sweet when she called. With people like Mr. Sweet, you didn't want to say the wrong thing. She always preferred to write him letters so she could double-check everything.

But in this situation, if she wanted to see her horse tonight, she had to call him. She could only hope he would be at home or had a portable phone. *It's almost Christmastime. A lot of people hang around the house more than usual at this time of year. If I'm lucky...*

Using the calling card she'd borrowed from Dylan, she picked up the pay phone and started punching in numbers.

The phone rang a few times. "Lawrence Sweet," a gruff voice answered.

He was home! For a split second, Danielle could not think of a single thing to say. She just stood there holding the phone, completely tongue-tied.

"Um...hi, Mr. Sweet. This is Danielle Conners."

"Yes?" Mr. Sweet said, sounding as if he was trying to place the name with a face.

"You remember me, don't you...Redman's owner?" *Ugh!* Danielle thought. *I sound so dumb.*

"Oh, yes, now I remember," Mr. Sweet said. "My little night bandit."

Danielle cringed. Would she ever live down taking Redman from Mr. Sweet's barn that night? she wondered.

"Well, sir," Danielle continued, "I'm with Alec Ramsay right now. You know, the guy who rides that big racehorse named the Black?"

"I know who Ramsay is, Ms. Conners," Mr. Sweet said impatiently. "I heard he was working with a new colt out at your place."

"That's right. And well, sir, you see, we're on the road on our way south, and, uh, we're going to be driving right by Rocky Mount, and since that's where you said your camp was..."

She took a deep breath. "You did say that, didn't you, sir?"

"Yes."

"Well, I was just wondering, sir, if maybe we could stop by so I could see my horse...I mean, Redman, you know, just to say hi."

"The camp is closed for winter recess," Mr. Sweet said. There was a pause. "Alec Ramsay is with you, you say?"

"Yes, sir."

Suddenly, Mr. Sweet's tone seemed friendlier. "Hmm...I don't see why not. You'll have to speak with Mr. Llamas, the manager, of course. Tell him I said it's okay and to give me a call when you get here." There was another pause. "I'd be interested to hear what Alec Ramsay thinks of our little stable."

Boy, thought Danielle, *Mr. Sweet really must be feeling in the holiday spirit.* She'd never heard him sound this nice before.

She thanked Mr. Sweet about a thousand times until he finally said good-bye.

Next, Danielle called the camp's manager at the number that Mr. Sweet had given her. "Whatever Mr. Sweet says is fine with me," Mr. Llamas told her when Danielle asked for permission to stop by the camp. He gave her directions.

Danielle was about to burst, she was so happy. After she hung up, she couldn't resist jumping up and down a few times. A man filling his car with gas stared at her.

Calm down, Danielle told herself, quickly cutting short her celebratory jig. If her crazy last-minute plan to see Redman was going to work, *everything* had to be handled carefully, one step at a time. Danielle took another deep breath. *Now for Alec,* she thought.

Alec came outside after paying the gas station attendant. He closed his wallet and tucked it into his pocket. "Ready to go, Danielle?" he said.

What should I say? Danielle asked herself. She was glad Dylan was still in the van with the horses and wouldn't hear this. But hadn't Alec himself made the suggestion to visit Redman?

"Sure, I'm ready," Danielle said. "But hey, Alec,

remember what we were talking about before? About me seeing Redman? I just talked with Mr. Sweet, and Mr. Llamas, the camp manager, too. Both gave us the okay to stop there, if you want. It's only a couple of miles from the highway. And Mr. Sweet said he'd like to know what you thought of the place. How about it? Can we stop by?"

Alec walked toward the driver's side of the van, with Danielle at his heels. "Did he tell you where this place is?" Alec asked.

"Mr. Llamas gave me directions how to get there. The camp is closed down for the winter break. It's just him living there with the horses right now."

Alec opened the van door but didn't get in. He looked at Danielle and frowned. "I don't know, Danielle," he said. "You saw what happened back at Aqueduct with Stedman's colt, didn't you? We have to be careful. We're carrying a van full of high-priced horseflesh, and they're all fillies besides."

"I know," Danielle said softly.

Alec took a deep breath. "What about the camp horses? Just being in the vicinity of a vanload of mares and fillies can drive some horses crazy."

Danielle nodded. "I asked Mr. Llamas about that. He said he didn't think there would be any trouble. The only horses at the camp right now are easy riders, like Redman."

"More like stable ponies, huh?" Alec was trying to be open-minded.

"That's right." Suddenly, Danielle couldn't help but break down and beg. "Come on, Alec. *Please?*" she said. "Who knows when I'm going to get a chance to see Redman again?" She glanced toward the back of the van, *really* glad Dylan wasn't there now.

Alec shrugged and swung up into the driver's seat. "Okay, Danielle," he said easily. "I'd planned on stopping in Rocky Mount, or somewhere along the road near there, anyway. Henry will probably kill me, but there's no way I'm going to make this drive all in one shot. Let's see how we feel when we cross the North Carolina border."

Yes! Danielle thought she might burst from happiness. She just knew Alec would say yes. He had to.

CHAPTER EIGHT

Reunion Time

The next few hours seemed like the longest Danielle had ever spent in her life. She couldn't believe her luck. For the last couple of months, she would have given anything to see her horse again. And now it was actually going to happen. In a little while they'd be in Rocky Mount.

The horses in the van were still quiet in their stalls. Some of them had nodded off standing up long ago. As Alec had predicted, it was an easy job. So far, at least. About all Danielle and Dylan had to do was give each of the fillies a few sips of warm water every once in a while. For most of the trip, Danielle gazed out the window, daydreaming about Redman. Dylan fiddled around with a couple of pieces of rope, trying to figure out some knots Alec was trying to teach him.

As the miles dragged by, the signs for different towns and cities passed almost without Danielle's seeing them. It sure wasn't anything like flying over New York City at night. Mostly it was just miles of boring interstate highway.

They passed Baltimore and Washington, then drove through Virginia, which seemed endless. When they reached the North Carolina state line, Alec stopped at a welcome center so they could all use the bathroom. As they were about to get back on the road, Alec gestured for Danielle to sit up front with him. "Bring the directions," he instructed.

Danielle's heart jumped. *They were going to see Redman for sure!* She patted her jacket. "I have them right in my pocket."

"Good," Alec said, then called over his shoulder, "Don't fall asleep back there, Dylan. Be ready, okay? Just in case something unexpected happens on these back roads."

"I won't fall asleep," Dylan said. He sounded slightly miffed that *he* was stuck in the back while his kid sister sat up front, riding shotgun.

Danielle made the big jump up into the passenger seat. She was so happy, she probably could have jumped over the Empire State Building. Alec turned the key, and the engine sparked to life. "All set?"

Danielle gave him a huge smile. "You bet!"

They pulled back onto the highway. When they reached the sign for Rocky Mount, Danielle followed the instructions she'd written down and told Alec where to turn off the interstate.

"It's pretty country around here," Alec said, noting the wide green pastures. Danielle gazed out into the distance. The late-afternoon sun was starting to sink to the horizon. But she didn't care about the scenery. All she cared about was Redman.

"Listen, Danielle, you watch yourself with Redman, okay?" Alec said softly. "I understand how anxious you are to see him. But a lot can happen with a horse in a month or six weeks or however long it's been. Things may have changed between you and him."

"I'll be careful," Danielle said, even though she didn't really understand what Alec meant. *How could anything change between me and Redman?* Though it seemed like forever, she and Redman hadn't been apart *that* long. In spirit, she'd never left him at all. But by now she'd learned enough from Alec Ramsay to know that when he spoke about horses, it was a good idea to listen.

Alec gave a little shrug and leaned on the wheel. "Hey, just a thought. He's your horse. You do what you think is right."

Danielle nodded again, but her eyes were straining to read a street sign: DEVON HILLS ROAD.

"That's it, Alec!" Danielle said joyfully. She glanced down at her directions again. "The camp is supposed to be at the end of this road."

Just to be safe in the fading sunlight, Alec switched on his headlights as they made their way along the county road that led to the Brookside Riding School—and Redman.

Danielle followed the street numbers anxiously. As they came closer to 600 Devon Hills Road, she looked over at Alec. "Um, Alec," she began hesitantly. "You know, I really appreciate what you're doing. Everything changed with Mr. Sweet when I told him I was with you."

Alec smiled but kept his eyes on a bend in the road ahead. Fenced pastureland stretched away on either side of the road. They passed the prestigious Brookside Academy, the boarding school to which the riding camp was attached. Then they followed the lane toward two long horse barns. The grounds were immaculately kept, Danielle noticed. Not a fence rail was out of place. The riding rings and paddocks looked like lawns in the early twilight.

"Is this it?" Dylan called from the back.

"Yeah," Danielle answered.

"Looks pretty fancy." Dylan seemed impressed.

"Hey, look at that," Alec said, pointing past one of the barns. "Isn't that your guy over there in that pasture?"

Danielle blinked. It *was* Redman. He was right there in front of her eyes!

Alec stopped the van and nodded toward the door. "Go on, get out," he said with a grin. "Go see your horse."

In a flash, Danielle was out the door and running to Redman.

Spirit of the Season

Danielle stopped at the fence and stood motionless, just watching her horse. Redman was all by himself, pulling up snatches of grass from a spot by the fence in the opposite corner of the pasture. *It's amazing to see him,* Danielle thought. She had missed him so much, and now he was right there. For real.

For an instant, she thought of what Alec had said about a horse changing over time and how things might be different now between her and Redman. That awful idea bounced around inside her mind like a Ping-Pong ball.

Better be careful, Danielle told herself. *Take it slow.* She placed one foot on the bottom fence rail and boosted herself up to sit on the top rail.

From up there, Redman looked the same as she remembered him: the same stocky build, the same red coat splotched with dabs of white, the same eye-patch markings on his face. He was her Redman, all

59

right. The one and only. He looked healthy enough, she decided. Maybe his stay at Mr. Sweet's riding camp hadn't been so terrible after all.

Redman stopped his grazing and lifted his head to watch Danielle as she started out through the pasture to meet him. She felt around inside her jacket and found the broken carrot pieces she had pocketed from her airplane dinner last night. She'd figured then that some horse along the way would appreciate them, and last night she had had only the faintest hope that the horse might be her Redman.

Danielle moved closer. She could clearly see the pirate patch over Redman's left eye. The last speck of sunlight glistened on his reddish brown spotted coat. Danielle held her breath as Redman began pawing the grass at his feet. Her hands shook. *This is it,* she told herself.

And then there was Redman, standing right in front of her. She could see the light of recognition spark in his eyes. Danielle's heart jumped. "You beautiful thing," she crooned softly. She reached up to touch the horse's neck. Redman lowered his head and began nudging her pockets. Danielle reached inside her jacket again and fed him one of the carrot pieces, feeling the tickle of warm breath and whiskers, the tongue wetting the palm of her hand. Tears welled in her eyes as she watched him eat.

Ordinarily, she would have let her horse finish snacking in peace, but this wasn't an ordinary occasion. Throwing her arms around Redman's neck, Danielle rubbed her face against his warm, soft coat. Immediately, the touch and smell of her old horse brought back a thousand memories, each one telling her that everything was going to be okay.

Redman quickly broke away from Danielle's embrace and turned into the wind.

"Come on now, Redman," Danielle said. "Don't be angry with me."

The paint tossed his head, his long red foretop dropping over his eyes. Then, with a snort, he threw his head in the air again and uttered a long neigh. He stood still a moment, tense and rigid. Then he turned to face Danielle. The paint's gaze settled on her, and once again she saw the familiar warmth in his large eyes. "Hey, you have to believe me, big guy. I didn't want you to leave," she told him. "It wasn't my fault that..."

But as the words came out of her mouth, Danielle realized how shallow they sounded. *Whose fault was it, then?* she scolded herself.

In truth, Danielle knew, Redman might never have been forced to leave Wishing Wells if she hadn't been so impulsive and run off with him from Mr. Sweet's barn that night. By taking matters into her own hands, she had *really* messed everything up.

If only she had just toughed it out… *Oh, shut up,* she told herself. *It wasn't all my fault. We were moving to the coast and Mom said we couldn't afford to bring Redman with us.* She shuddered at the memory of that awful time. What would have happened if Alec Ramsay hadn't walked into their lives back then?

Reaching up, Danielle gave the paint a rub on the forehead and scratched him behind his ears. He'd always liked that. Suddenly, to her surprise he sprang back on his haunches, half rearing and pulling away from her. His eyes grew larger, and she could see the whites around their edges.

"Easy, big guy," she soothed. "Easy now."

That's funny, Danielle thought. *Why doesn't he want me to scratch behind his ears?* Maybe the kids at the camp had been overdoing the ear scratching and nose patting.

Redman cantered off to the opposite side of the pasture. Danielle called softly to her horse. The paint did not respond. Danielle called louder and louder, feeling almost desperate. Finally, Redman sniffed the air, then came trotting forward with head and tail high. Danielle reached out to him. This time, the horse did not move away at her touch. Unable to stop herself, Danielle threw her arms around him again and buried her head in his long mane. He rested his chin on Danielle's shoulder and whuffled softly in her ear.

Just then, a man in a fur-lined parka and hiking boots appeared at the pasture gate. As he came closer to Danielle and Redman, Danielle could hear him muttering to himself, "Sure could use a dose of orange juice and sunshine myself. I have half a mind to catch a ride in that van, too."

Danielle wasn't sure what to make of that. *Who is this guy, anyway?* she thought nervously.

The man gave Danielle a nod. "Hello! Are you the one who's come for Red?"

Come for Red? Danielle didn't know what to make of that, either.

"Hi," she said. "I mean, yes, I've come to see him," she said. "Are you Mr. Llamas?"

"That's right," the man replied. He began to fix Redman with a halter and lead line.

"Come on, Red," he said. It was weird to see someone else handle her horse with such familiarity, Danielle thought. Mr. Llamas clucked to the paint and started to lead Redman toward the barn. Danielle followed and fell in step beside them.

"Mr. Sweet wanted me to call when we got here. I didn't have a chance…" she began.

The manager chuckled. "He's on the phone right now with your friend Alec the jockey, talking his ear off. My boss is a big racetrack fan." He led Redman from the paddock into a barn. It was one of several long, narrow buildings, with a low, peaked roof. The barn had a center aisle and at least ten box stalls along both sides. Most of the stalls were empty.

Alec was on the phone in the office at one end of the barn, laughing. When he spotted Danielle, he nodded for her to come closer.

"Here she is now," Alec said to the person on the other end. "Why don't you tell her?"

Tell me what? Danielle thought.

Alec handed the phone to her.

"Hello?" she said cautiously.

"Danielle, this is Lawrence Sweet again. I've been speaking with Mr. Ramsay. He said there was a bit of extra room in the van he's driving south, and he suggested that it would be in the spirit of the season to take that horse to Florida for the holidays."

Redman? To Wishing Wells? Danielle figured she wasn't hearing right.

"Under the circumstances," Mr. Sweet continued, "with you being here and the camp being closed until after the new year, I don't see why not."

Danielle could barely speak. "Bring Redman all the way to Florida? You mean it?" she practically croaked.

"Mr. Ramsay vouches for you and says I can trust you. I hope so. I know we've had our problems before, young lady, but I might be prepared to put all that behind us."

Danielle swallowed. This was better than she could ever have dared to hope for. Her fingers tightened on the receiver, and she looked at Alec, still in shock. He smiled and winked at her.

"However, there *is* one thing," Mr. Sweet said. His voice sounded cautious now. "The animal must be back here in Rocky Mount before camp starts again. I wanted to speak to you personally and make sure you understood that."

"Y-yes, sir," Danielle stammered.

"Again, that horse is to be back here by the start of the new year. Those are the conditions under which Redman may leave. Agreed?"

Danielle took hold of herself. "Agreed. Absolutely. I mean, thank you very much. He'll be back whenever you say, I promise."

"Good."

Danielle felt dizzy—everything was happening so fast. She turned the phone back over to Alec, who listened to Mr. Sweet for a minute and smiled. "Sure, I'd be glad to," he said. "Happy holidays to you, too." He hung up and looked at Danielle.

"Is this really true? Redman can come home with us?" she asked.

"Merry Christmas, Danielle," Alec said. "And don't say I never did anything for you, okay?"

"I can't believe this!" Danielle gasped, the situation finally sinking in. "Thank you so, so much. You don't know what this means to me."

Alec waved toward the door. "Go and get one of the Hopeful Farm stable blankets from the van, will you, Danielle?"

Danielle jumped up joyfully and ran to the van. Dylan was sitting with the horses, reading a comic book. She told him about Redman. Her brother seemed as stunned as she had been by Mr. Sweet's generous offer.

"It must have been because of Alec," Danielle went on, opening one of the tack trunks and looking for a stable blanket in the traditional Hopeful Farm colors. "Mr. Sweet seemed really impressed. Sometimes I forget Alec is as famous as he is, at least with horse people. Mr. Sweet really is acting sweet today."

Dylan nodded. "Well, that's great, D. Boy, will Mom and Dad be surprised," was all he said. But Danielle knew that her brother understood what having Redman home even for a little while meant to her.

Danielle found what she was looking for and headed back to the barn. When she handed the blanket to Alec, he laid it on a table and scrawled something in black marker under the Hopeful Farm logo. When Danielle peered over his shoulder, she saw that the words read: "To all the riders at Camp

Brookside, Happy trails, Alec Ramsay."

Danielle grinned. Mr. Sweet had traded nearly two whole weeks with Redman for Alec Ramsay's autograph!

That seemed like a great deal to her.

CHAPTER TEN

Musical Stalls

"Knuckleheads!" Alec called to Danielle and Dylan inside the van. "Come on, you two. Let's get these ladies outside."

Dylan poked his head out of the van and gave Alec a surprised look. "What's going on?"

Alec shrugged. "Hey, like I said, I'm not driving all night if I don't have to. Mr. Sweet said we could stay overnight at the camp. And our lodging is free. Sounds good to me."

Boy, thought Danielle, *Mr. Sweet sure was feeling pretty generous, all right.*

Alec and Dylan brought the horses into the barn just as Danielle and Mr. Llamas were finishing preparing the stalls. Soon, after they had tossed in a couple of armloads of hay for bedding and spread it around, each one of Alec's fillies had her own roomy stall ready to sleep in.

Dylan and Danielle were given stable cots so they

could bed down with the horses in the barn, while Alec was offered an extra bedroom in Mr. Llamas's cottage.

"Are you guys hungry?" Alec asked after the horses were taken care of. "I'll get some pizza and sodas delivered."

Dylan perked up a bit. "Sure, that'd be great."

"Okay," Alec said, "I'll call in the order."

He went with Mr. Llamas to see where he was going to sleep. Danielle and Dylan unfolded their cots beside a little electric heater in the barn's tack room. It was dark by now and the temperature was dropping.

Stepping out into the aisle a little while later, Danielle thought she heard a familiar whinny. *That's Reddy*, she told herself. Walking toward the other end of the barn, she passed the fillies and a few of the camp's ponies and riding horses. Dim bulbs burned high on the ceiling above, casting the stalls in dark shadows. *A strange barn sure can seem spooky at night,* she thought.

Danielle moved quietly so as not to disturb any of the horses who were lying down. A few of the others put their heads over their stall doors. Alec had fed and tucked the fillies in for the night, each with a new winter blanket.

When she reached Redman's stall, she found the paint nosing around his hay rack. "Redman," she called to him softly.

He recognized her voice, even at a whisper. He stretched his neck and came over to the door. She reached out, and Redman blew on her fingers. "Good boy," she said. "Sorry. I don't have any more treats for you right now." He nickered, then put his muzzle up to her cheek and blew softly down the back of her collar. She ruffled his mane and fussed over him with a brush. Her uneasy feeling was fading.

Just then, a pizza guy arrived with two pizzas, one veggie and one pepperoni. Alec was right behind him. He paid the deliveryman, opened one of the boxes, and picked up a slice of pizza. He looked like he was in a hurry.

"Hi," Danielle said. "Thanks for the food."

"Sure." Alec glanced around anxiously. It was plain to see he had more on his mind than food.

"Is something wrong, Alec?" Danielle asked.

"Yeah, I'm afraid so. We're going to have to break out of here, sorry to say. You and Dylan need to fold up your cots."

"What?" Dylan said, his eyes widening. He had just come over, attracted by the delicious smell of pizza.

"But we just got the horses bedded down!" Danielle said. "I thought you said we were staying the night."

Alec shook his head. "Henry tracked us down," he

said, between bites of pizza. "Stupid cell phone. That's what I get for charging up my batteries, I guess. Anyway, he's down in Florida already and none too pleased to hear we are still in North Carolina."

"He really wants you to drive all night?" Danielle asked.

Alec shrugged. "Henry gets nervous sometimes when our horses are on the road. And this is one of those times."

Danielle nodded, wondering if she and Dylan weren't two of the reasons Henry was so anxious.

"Anyway," Alec said, "he wants us down there fast. Like, *right now*. Looks like I'm going to be driving all night, after all."

Danielle and Dylan looked at each other.

Alec gave a little sigh and gobbled up the last of his slice. "There's no way out of it, I guess. When Henry says move, we move." He wiped his face and hands with a napkin, then nodded to Danielle and Dylan. "Come on, then. We can take the rest of the pizza with us. Let's load up. We'd better get back on the road."

A moment later, Mr. Llamas came into the barn and started opening stall doors. He didn't look too happy about the game of musical stalls they'd been playing all evening. A few of the horses were also a little cranky at having their sleep interrupted, but finally the fillies and Redman were safely in the van.

Alec thanked Mr. Llamas and apologized for the mix-up.

"Just tell me one thing," Mr. Llamas asked Alec before they left. "Is the Black really as wild as they say? I've only seen him race on TV, and they always have to take so many precautions. He never seems to be in the post parade. Does he always have to go to the gate by himself?"

"Not always," Alec said. "It depends. He's a fighter, that's for sure. Some people think he shouldn't even be racing, that he's half crazy."

"But you know him better than anyone," Mr. Llamas pressed. "What's he really like, to you?"

"To me?" Alec smiled. "Well, to put it simply, I don't know what I'd do without the Black. He's my best friend."

Mr. Llamas gave Alec a funny look.

Alec laughed. "Sorry," he said. "Sometimes people think it's kind of funny when I say that about a horse. But I guess it's true. If there is one thing I know in this life, it's that I can count on the Black and he can count on me."

That's just how I feel about Redman, thought Danielle.

"Yep," Mr. Llamas said, nodding slowly. "That's a friend, no doubt about it."

"Okay, guys," Alec said, jumping into the van's driver's seat and putting his key in the ignition.

"Let's spark it up and hit the highway." Danielle and Dylan ran around the van, jumped in, and took their places in the rear seats.

Back on the road, Danielle and Dylan took turns checking on the horses every twenty minutes or so. A couple of them were a little restless. Redman was asleep, so Danielle let him be. It was getting a lot colder. Danielle adjusted the blankets on the horses, making sure they all were warm and covered up.

Dylan was fidgeting in his seat, seeming as restless as the horses. "You know what this means, don't you?" he said.

"What?" Danielle asked.

Dylan frowned. "If Alec is driving straight through, we won't be able to stop and see Dad tomorrow."

"Oh, no!" Danielle gasped. What her brother had said was true. A pang of sadness shot through her heart.

Mr. Conners was touring the South with his band right now: Nashville, New Orleans, Muscle Shoals. He'd been home only for short visits a couple of times in the past few months. Danielle really missed her dad. The last she'd heard from him, the band was looking for a new drummer. Sometimes she wished they'd find a replacement for her dad, too.

"Let's try calling Dad at the next gas station," Dylan said finally. "I have the phone number of the place where he's playing tonight."

Danielle nodded. "Sounds good. Hey, maybe we can meet for a few minutes somewhere near the interstate."

"We can sure try," Dylan said.

Getting to see their dad was one of the big reasons that her brother had decided to come along on this trip, Danielle knew. There was no way he would give up on that idea easily.

Alec lent Dylan his phone and called their dad. Luckily, Mr. Conners was in between sets and able to come to the phone. Dylan explained where they were, and after quickly talking it over with Alec, he arranged to meet at a truck stop on the highway outside Macon, a diner named the Seville.

"All right!" Dylan said excitedly, flipping the phone closed and passing it through the partition to Alec. "Thanks, Alec."

"I knew we could figure something out," Danielle said.

"Well, your mom told me you guys were counting on this," Alec said sleepily. "We're going to have to stop and eat anyway. It'll be late, though," he warned. "Probably close to four in the morning by the time we get there."

Danielle didn't care, just as long as she could see her dad. And she was certain Dad felt the same way. Being up that late might have been a little uncomfortable for some dads, but not hers. He was used to working at night.

"And we can't stay too long," Alec cautioned them.

"We know," Dylan said, nodding. "But it'll be worth it."

"Thanks, Alec," Danielle said gratefully.

The miles rolled by. Every once in a while, drafts of freezing cold air wafted through the vents in the van. Danielle huddled deeper into her jacket. She hadn't expected it to be so chilly in South Carolina.

Dylan pointed out the window to a group of lit-up signs along the highway advertising fireworks for sale. South Carolina was one of the few states in the country where fireworks were legal.

"I wish we could stop here so I could pick up some supplies," Dylan said.

"Yeah, right," Danielle snorted. "Alec would just love that, I bet."

"You'd probably tell him, too, you little snitch," Dylan said.

Danielle smiled. She wasn't really a snitch. She knew plenty of things about Dylan that Mom or Dad would like to know, and she never ratted him out—unless it was absolutely necessary, of course.

After what seemed like endless dark miles, they arrived at the truck stop outside Macon, in central Georgia. They were right on schedule, at 3:55 A.M.

At least two dozen trucks were parked in the wide parking area beyond the fuel pumps. The Seville Diner was obviously a favorite late-night meeting place for long-haulers with their monstrous eighteen-wheel rigs. A neon sign buzzing out front said: THE SEVILLE DINER—OPEN 24 HOURS.

Alec pulled the van right up in front of the diner's plate-glass window, as close as he could get to the entrance. He offered to stay with the horses so Danielle and Dylan could both see their dad at the same time. Settling onto one of the benches in the back of the van, he kicked up his feet and stretched out with a cup of coffee from his thermos.

"Go ahead, you two," he said, nodding toward the door. "But bring me some fresh coffee and an order of scrambled eggs, potatoes, and toast, will you?"

"You got it, Alec," Danielle said, giving him a mock salute. Then she raced toward the entrance of the diner, running as fast as her legs would take her. She was almost tripping over herself, she was so happy.

Danielle hadn't been expecting any of this a few days ago. Now she had Redman back, at least for a while, and she was about to see her dad, too.

Could things *ever* be any better?

•

Early-Morning Emergency

As Danielle came through the door, heads turned and everyone stared. A twelve-year-old girl coming into a place like the Seville Diner at four in the morning must have been a big surprise to all the regulars, she figured.

Danielle didn't care. Her dad was in here somewhere. And Dylan was right behind her. She looked around and quickly spotted her dad sitting on a stool near the end of the counter.

"Hey, Dad!" Danielle called, running toward him. Mr. Conners stood up from his stool and welcomed her with a smile and open arms. He must have come straight from the club because he was still wearing his stage gear, a flashy black-fringed cowboy shirt with pearl buttons and embroidered parrots and roses.

Danielle flew into his arms like a bird landing in a nest. He swept her off her feet with a big bear hug.

"Who is this beautiful young lady?" he said. The other customers smiled.

As soon as her dad put her down, he gave Dylan a bear hug, too. Finally, they all squeezed into a booth. As they talked, Danielle kept looking at her father and brother together. You could really see the family resemblance between them these days—the same lanky build, broad shoulders, high cheekbones, and reddish blond hair.

Across the aisle, sitting at the counter with big breakfast plates in front of them, were two of the guys from her dad's band, Jack Tagger and Clyde Katz. They were talking to each other but looking over every now and then at Danielle and Dylan. Danielle wondered whether they had families they missed back home. Life on the road could be tough sometimes.

Suddenly, Clyde bugged out his eyes behind his thick black-framed glasses and made a funny face at Danielle. She had to laugh. Clyde played pedal steel guitar and had been with the band the longest. He was a real joker and had known Danielle ever since she was little. Jack Tagger played bass and had been in the band for years, too. Like Danielle's dad, they wore western-cut shirts, jeans, and boots.

Mr. Conners began asking Danielle and Dylan all sorts of questions, about their trip, their school, and their mom.

"Mom's fine," Dylan said. "She's working a lot, though."

Mr. Conners looked sad for a moment. "Is that so? I hope you kids are taking good care of her." Just then, the waitress came up with menus, and the three of them ordered a hearty meal of eggs, grits, sausage, bacon, potatoes, and orange juice.

Danielle told her dad about Alec being stuck out in the van, and Mr. Conners ordered him a plate of eggs and potatoes and a large container of fresh coffee and asked that the food be delivered to the horse van.

Time passed almost before they knew it. When Danielle glanced over toward the counter, she caught Clyde signaling to her dad, tapping his watch.

She looked at her dad apologetically. "We have to go, too," she said slowly.

Her dad reached for his wallet. "My schedule is so messed up these days, I guess we were just lucky to see each other at all." He smiled and ruffled Dylan's hair. "We have to make it to Mobile by noon tomorrow, then come back here two days later." He shook his head. "It's too much. But things will get better soon, kids. I promise."

Danielle and Dylan leaned in against either side of their dad.

"Oh, I almost forgot," Mr. Conners said. He reached under the table and pulled out a brown paper bag. Then he took two gift-wrapped boxes out of the bag.

"Go ahead," he said. "Open them."

Danielle glanced around the diner, feeling a little embarrassed. By now it seemed as if practically everybody in the Seville was watching them. It was like having Christmas onstage.

But she couldn't complain. She was just glad to be here. In about two minutes, she would be leaving with her horses, and her dad would be on his way to Mobile with the band. There wasn't time to be shy.

They opened their presents: riding boots for Danielle and a black belt with a silver buckle for Dylan. "We have presents for you, too," Dylan said. From his pocket he pulled a key chain with a scorpion on it. Danielle gave her dad a harmonica.

"This is great, kids," Mr. Conners said. "But what matters the most is that we're together right now. That's the best present I could ask for."

"I love you, Dad," Danielle said, kissing him on the cheek.

"I love you, too, sweetheart."

They all got up. Mr. Conners left some money with the check, then stretched and rubbed his neck. Danielle looked at the clock. It was almost five A.M.

As Danielle and Dylan headed toward the door, their dad suddenly frowned and blocked their way with his arm. "Hold on a second," he said, giving a little nod to his left.

Danielle glanced in the direction of the cash register. Three loud, scruffy-looking guys were arguing about something with the waitress and another woman who was probably the manager.

A big, rough-looking trucker stood up from the counter and stepped over to stand beside the waitress. Then two burly men came out of the kitchen. One of them held a long wooden rolling pin in his hand. At a nod from the manager, the big men escorted the three rowdies outside and into the parking lot, then came back inside.

Mr. Conners seemed to ignore the whole thing. "We'll just stay in here for a few minutes," he told Danielle and her brother calmly. Her dad saw lots of arguments and bar fights in his job, Danielle knew. He'd told her many times that you couldn't work the club circuit and *not* see people getting into trouble once in a while.

To Danielle, the whole thing was a little scary. She, Dylan, and their dad went back and joined Clyde and Jack at the counter. Clyde began to kid with her, putting a napkin on his head and making funny faces, trying to get her to laugh.

Suddenly, there was even more commotion out front, with yelling and the sound of motorcycles zooming away.

And smoke.

"Fire!" Danielle heard someone yell. The manager lady was doing a crazy dance by the cash register. She seemed to be kicking at something on the floor. *What's going on?* Danielle wondered.

People scrambled for the door as puffs of heavy smoke started spreading in clouds through the diner.

There must be a fire in the kitchen, Danielle thought. She turned to her father. "Shouldn't we get out of here?" she asked.

Mr. Conners was sniffing at the smoke. "Sulfur," he said coolly. "That's no fire. It's a smoke bomb."

Jack got up from his stool and shook his head. "Stupid jerks," he said, and quietly counted out some coins. He casually laid his tip on the counter as if nothing out of the ordinary was happening.

Danielle blinked a couple of times as her eyes began to water a little. The smoke was starting to sting them. "Let's go," her dad said, and holding their sleeves over their mouths to filter out the smoke, they walked toward the door.

Dylan suddenly grabbed Danielle's arm. "Look!" he said, pointing through the window.

She glanced through the plate glass out into the parking lot. Under the bright lights outside, she could see Alec and two truckers chasing a pair of horses across the parking lot. Danielle blinked again.

Was she seeing things? Horses running loose in the parking lot?

She gasped, fear snapping her awake.

"Those are Alec's horses!" she cried. "How did they get out of the van?"

"We have to do something," Dylan said.

Danielle began to panic. What if one of Alec's horses got hurt? Each one was worth many thousands of dollars. *And where was Redman?*

One man had a couple of horses by their halters and was waving at a crowd of gawkers for help. Danielle squinted, looking closer. One of the horses the man was holding was Maradona—and the other was Redman! The man was doing his best to calm the horses, but he was barely keeping them under control.

Danielle ran through the door. Her father took her by the hand and started pushing through a knot of coughing truckers, trying to get fresh air.

Out in the parking lot, the Hopeful Farm horse van was awash in smoke. The back doors of the van were open. People and horses were rushing around and the parking lot was in complete chaos.

As the people crowded together, Danielle heard someone saying, "…then Elvira kicked that smoke bomb right out the door. So it rolls across the way and under that big horse van, where some half-asleep trucker on his way to get a cup of coffee sees it and thinks the van's on fire and decides to be a hero. He set them horses loose."

"Never a dull moment at the Seville, huh?" someone else said.

Danielle looked around wildly. *Where were Alec and Redman now?*

Roundup!

Alec's fillies were still wheeling around the parking lot like acrobats. It was as if a circus act had gone berserk.

With the smoke bomb and all the commotion with the horses, practically everyone who had been in the Seville was in the parking lot by now. So many people were trying to help round up the runaways that it almost made matters worse. Most of the men didn't seem to know anything about horses, especially what to do in a situation like this. They were just frightening the animals by waving their arms and yelling. Mr. Conners, Clyde, and Jack ran after them to get them to stop.

Redman, Danielle thought. *Where is he now? Is he okay?* She was about to head toward the spot she'd last seen him when something made her stop.

Against the side of the diner, five people were

spread out, trying to corner Severlite, the youngest bay filly. She was already very keyed up, and the people trying to corner her weren't helping the situation.

"Dylan," Danielle said quickly. "Can you go find the guy who has Redman and that other horse? I have to try to help with Severlite over here."

Ordinarily, Dylan would never have let his kid sister order him around. But this situation was different. Aside from Alec and their dad, Danielle probably knew more about horses than anyone else in the parking lot, and Dylan knew it.

"Go on, Dylan," Danielle said impatiently. "Hurry up. Run!"

A horse shrilled loudly. Dylan pushed past a couple of gawkers and dashed off. Danielle turned to see her dad, Jack, and Clyde chasing the gray filly, Ninadja, away from the street that led back to the highway. *Thank goodness,* she thought.

Danielle took a breath and ran over to see if she could help with Severlite. The filly was thrashing around and rearing up, keeping everyone at a distance. She was backed into a corner and feeling trapped. Danielle could see the whites of her eyes shining with terror in the gleam of the streetlights. Her legs were braced, and she blasted a fiery snort at the person nearest to her, a heavy guy with a mustache. Danielle stepped past him and called Severlite by name, keeping her voice soft and reassuring.

Severlite waited until Danielle was just a finger's length from her, then spun around and ran past mustache man, who dove out of the way to keep from getting trampled. Danielle had half expected the filly to wheel and was chasing right after her the instant Severlite bolted.

For the next few minutes, Danielle dodged back and forth. Finally, she was able to catch up to Severlite, move to her head, and take hold of her forelock. It was the best Danielle could do, as the filly seemed to have slipped her halter somehow.

"Easy now, girl," Danielle said. "Easy. That's it, be nice now."

She continued to grip the filly's foretop tightly, waiting for an explosion from the horse that could come at any second. Danielle didn't know what she might do if Severlite started really bucking and rearing.

The filly snorted again. Danielle eased her around, keeping up a flow of gentle talk. A few moments later, the young filly was still restless but beginning to settle down at last. Danielle led her cautiously back to the van.

While she had been playing her dodging game with Severlite, it looked as if Alec and the others had managed to round up all the other runaways and get them back inside the van.

Well, almost all.

Danielle quickly realized that one horse remained loose: the black filly, Darsky. On the far side of the van, she could see Alec trying to take her in hand. Darsky was bucking and playing and hadn't the slightest intention of getting back in the van. Mr. Conners and a few other men were standing at a respectful distance, watching Alec try to calm the filly.

Danielle turned Severlite over to Dylan and Clyde and went to join her dad. She wasn't sure there was anything she could do to help with Darsky. Alec was amazingly calm, but the filly had gone from excited to angry. She was dancing in short, stumbling steps, shaking and snorting, blowing and rolling her eyes.

Suddenly, the filly panicked. She bolted straight at the diner and plowed into a head-high hedge between the sidewalk and the plate-glass window.

Caught half in, half out of the brushy hedge, Darsky gave a bellowing neigh, pawing at the ground with her right hoof, which had poked through the far side of the hedge. Danielle and her dad started toward the filly, but Alec waved them and everyone else back.

Hurrying around the side of the hedge and moving quickly to the filly's head, Alec managed to get her steadied just in time. Soon he had Darsky picking her way backward onto the sidewalk. She kept up a chorus of neighs and whinnies, but with Alec's hands on her, she slowly calmed down. Finally, he was able to get her back to the van without further incident. Incredibly, Darsky's only injury seemed to be a few scratches on her legs where she'd run into the hedge.

After all the horses were loaded, the crowd in the parking lot slowly began to disperse. Alec thanked many of those who had tried to help and even some who hadn't.

Danielle stood at the door of the van with her dad, Clyde, Jack, and Dylan.

"Did anyone see who threw the smoke bomb?" Danielle asked.

"One of those bikers, I bet," Dylan said. "Didn't you hear them taking off right when everything started?"

"Oh, I wouldn't jump to conclusions," Clyde said. "It could have been anybody. Maybe some guy just didn't like his hamburger."

"But I heard them!" Dylan protested.

Jack shrugged. "There are lots of motorcycle riders around here, son," he said. "Especially the past few days. People were saying they're all going to a big biker weekend down in Daytona Beach."

"So it still could have been some of them," Dylan said stubbornly.

Clyde gave Dylan a friendly rap on the top of his head with his knuckles. "You're in biker country now, boy."

"Grow up, will you, Clyde?" Mr. Conners said, laughing as Clyde and Dylan punched shoulders and pretended to fight.

Finally, Alec finished his last thank-yous and came over.

Danielle's dad stepped forward with his hand out. "Good to see you, Alec."

Alec looked tired, but managed a smile. "Likewise, Mr. Conners."

"Seeing my kids like this means a lot, Mr. Ramsay. I really want to thank you. I know you're on a tight schedule."

"My pleasure, sir," Alec said. He glanced at the van and mopped the sweat from his brow with his shirtsleeve.

"So what happened, Alec?" Danielle asked.

Alec sighed. "I guess I fell asleep after I ate all that food. The next thing I knew, when I opened my eyes, there was smoke everywhere and some guys were yelling 'Fire!' and trying to pull me out the door. I thought I was having some kind of nightmare!"

"It was just a smoke bomb, Alec," Danielle said.

"So I hear," Alec said grimly. "I hope whoever set it off had fun."

"They threw it into the diner first," Danielle explained. "Then someone kicked it outside and it rolled under the van."

"Well, everything sure happened fast," Alec said. "But no real damage done. Luckily," he added under his breath. He clapped his hands and looked at Danielle and Dylan. "Okay, gang. The road beckons. We have to be on our way."

After a few more hugs for Danielle and Dylan, Mr. Conners followed Jack and Clyde to the big white Cadillac they had borrowed from the guy who owned the club where they were playing that evening.

Danielle sighed as she watched them pull out of the parking lot, wondering when she would see her dad again. Hopefully at Christmas, if he didn't have a gig. She climbed into the back of the van as Alec cranked up the engine.

What else will happen before this crazy trip is over? she wondered.

For now, at least, the horses were quiet. All the late-night excitement must have worn them out.

I'm *worn out*, Danielle thought. *How long will this peace and quiet last?*

❦ CHAPTER THIRTEEN ❧

Biker Country

"Danielle," Alec called through the partition about half an hour later, "go back and check on Darsky, will you?"

"Right," Danielle said. She got up and stepped down the aisle separating the stalls. Alec had cleaned the filly's scratches with some liquid soap but hadn't seemed too worried about them. He hadn't even used a bandage when he was through.

Danielle carefully slipped in beside the sleeping filly and crouched to inspect her leg. The cuts looked clean and dry.

"She's fine," Danielle called to Alec when she returned to her seat. "I guess we're lucky she didn't get hurt any worse than she did."

"You can say *that* again," Alec agreed. "On the other hand, horses are pretty strong. Steeplechasers run into hedges all the time."

"Maybe Darsky's trying to tell us something," Danielle said.

"Oh, yeah? Like what?" Alec asked.

"Like she wants to jump hedges," Danielle said.

"Well, if that's so, she didn't get off to a very good start," Alec said, with a sleepy laugh.

The sky was starting to lighten in the east, Danielle noticed. Gray light was filtering through the high window on the left side of the van. She took a deep breath and tried to wake herself up a bit. She was so tired. She couldn't remember the last time she'd stayed up all night. Whenever it was, the experience had been nothing like this. She felt sorry for Alec, having to drive. He was drinking cup after cup of coffee.

Danielle leaned back in her seat and stared bleary-eyed out the window, thinking about her dad and wondering where he was right now. On his way to Alabama, no doubt. She wondered if he really did like his harmonica. It was in the key of A major, his favorite. That was why she'd bought it.

They were still in Georgia, but every minute brought them closer to the Florida border. Soon they would be in Wishing Wells, and this crazy trip would be just a memory. Except for Redman, of course.

Danielle smiled to herself. She couldn't wait to get home and ride her horse again. Two whole weeks with her very own horse! She'd figure out how to get Redman back to Mr. Sweet's camp later. Much later. She didn't even want to think about that yet.

"I can't believe Alec was so cool about what happened back there," Dylan said. "I thought these horses were supposed to be so valuable and all."

"They are," Danielle assured her brother. "Maybe one of the reasons everything turned out okay was because Alec *didn't* lose his head when the horses escaped."

Dylan nodded. "I guess. But what is Henry Dailey going to say when he hears what happened to his fillies?"

Danielle groaned. She'd forgotten about Henry. "I hope he doesn't blame us somehow."

"Us?!" Dylan said. "What did *we* do?"

"Well, Alec wouldn't have stopped at that truck stop if it wasn't for us meeting up with Dad."

"Yeah," Dylan said, shrugging. "But hey, it could have happened anywhere."

Try telling that to Henry Dailey, Danielle thought.

The next time she checked on the horses, she found Redman still dozing peacefully in his stall. She brushed a fly away from his ear. Aside from a slight flicker, Redman didn't flinch. The fly buzzed around in a circle, then headed off to torment Maradona.

What a prince of a horse Redman was, Danielle thought proudly. During all the ruckus at the Seville he had given them the least trouble.

Suddenly, she heard a rumble coming from behind the van. Danielle ran back up to her seat to look out the window. The roaring outside grew louder.

"Bikers again!" Dylan said. His voice sounded both worried and awed.

Danielle pressed her face up against the glass. In the early-morning light she could see two leather-clad, long-haired, bearded guys on a pair of low-slung Harleys with slanting front forks and high handle-bars.

On their leather jackets, the bikers were wearing patches with the words "Unforgiven" and "Fayette-ville, SC." Right behind the first two bikers was another pair, then another. Soon the two lines of motorcycles started past the van, their engines growl-ing.

"I wonder if those are the guys who threw that smoke bomb into the Seville," Dylan said.

Danielle shrugged. "Give it up, Dylan."

"Could be," Dylan said. "They're from South Carolina, right? I bet they're carrying tons of fire-works."

Danielle had no idea why her brother was so sure that, of all the people in the world, these were the guys who had bombed the Seville and that they were loaded with fireworks to boot. But she was too tired to argue or even to remind him what Clyde had said about their being in biker country. Dylan could be very stubborn sometimes.

As the van slowly plowed on through the predawn light, more cars and trucks passed. So did pack after pack of motorcycle clubs. Some were in groups of twenty or more, others as small as two or three. Almost all the riders' jackets displayed what Dylan called their colors—the names of the clubs and where they came from. Some of the names were sort of interesting, Danielle thought. "Rampagers... Raleigh–Durham" was her favorite so far.

"Didn't Jack say there was some sort of biker convention going on in Daytona? We must be getting closer," Danielle said after the sixth or seventh pack went by.

"Looks like it," Dylan nodded.

"Ten miles to the Florida line," Alec called from up front.

Danielle lay back on her seat and sighed. They were almost home. She barely noticed as another pair of motorcycles pulled up on the left side of the van.

"Oggie!" she heard Alec shout. "Holy smokes!"

Suddenly, the van was slowing down. So were its motorcycle escorts. Danielle and Dylan jumped to the window. One biker drew alongside Alec, and the other pulled in front of the van.

What's going on? Danielle wondered nervously.

"We're being hijacked," Dylan whispered. "They want the horses." He started looking around and picked up a short-handled pitchfork to protect them with.

"Oh, please," Danielle said disgustedly. "You've been watching too many action movies. What's up, Alec?" she called through the partition, her voice shaking a bit.

Alec didn't answer for a moment. "Oh, nothing. I'm just going to stop and talk with this guy a minute."

Alec didn't sound worried, but what if Dylan was right? Could Alec be pretending to be calm so she and Dylan wouldn't panic? *No,* Danielle told herself. *He'd be much too afraid that we'd get hurt.* But who was this strange guy on the bike?

The van edged off to the side of the road and stopped. So did the motorcycles.

"Is everything all right back there?" Alec called to Danielle. "Everything's cool," she answered. *I hope,* she added to herself.

Some of the horses were waking up now and starting to get restless. The van had hit a few bumps slowing down, and a few of the horses had had to scramble to keep their balance.

"Good," Alec said. "Then sit tight. This will only take a second." He got out of the van, slamming the door.

Dylan was looking worried and still had a tight grip on his pitchfork. He was perched behind the door, just waiting for someone to start something. Danielle couldn't resist sneaking over to a window and peering outside.

The two bikers were walking toward Alec. It looked like a shoot-out at high noon in some old black-and-white Western on TV. They came closer and closer. When they were about ten feet from each other, they stopped. Alec's back was to Danielle, so she couldn't see his face. One of the bikers was saying something, but Danielle couldn't hear what.

"What's happening now?" Dylan asked.

"Shh!" Danielle told him. "I can't tell. They're talking about something."

Suddenly, Alec jumped forward. So did one of the bikers. *Oh, no!* Danielle thought. *This is it! They're going to fight it out!*

Danielle kept her eyes glued to the window, her hands balled into fists. She was ready to fight to defend her horses if she had to.

It looked like Alec and the biker were wrestling, but something about the way they were going about it puzzled Danielle.

They're not wrestling at all, she realized suddenly. *They're hugging!* Danielle laughed in relief.

"What's going on?" Dylan asked frantically.

"We're not being hijacked, Dylan," Danielle said, catching her breath. "Alec knows that guy!"

CHAPTER FOURTEEN

Mission Accomplished

"So who's that?" Danielle asked when Alec got back into the van.

Alec laughed. "That's good ol' Oggie Vargas. Looks like he turned in his horse for a bike."

"You *know* him?" Dylan said doubtfully. He sounded as if he was having a hard time believing that a famous jockey would be hanging out with a biker.

"Sure," Alec said. "Oggie used to work up at Saratoga, exercising horses in the morning and hustling rides in the afternoon."

"So he's a jockey, too?" Danielle asked.

"Yep. A good one. I haven't seen him for a long time, since just after I first started racing the Black. We were both apprentices then. Oggie's a real prankster. We used to have some good times together."

"Oh." Danielle looked at her brother and tapped

him on the shoulder, as if to say, "Hijacking—right." Dylan glanced away.

"It was incredible to run into him like this," Alec continued.

"Do many jockeys become bikers?" Dylan asked.

Alec laughed again. "I don't think so. Oggie's the only one I know."

When they finally crossed the Florida border, Danielle and Dylan slapped palms to congratulate each other. They were tired and worn out from the long, hard night, but they were almost home at last. Danielle recognized the radio station Alec was playing. They were really close now. Pretty soon they would be at South Wind and...

Henry!

Danielle couldn't put the crusty old trainer out of her mind. *What will he say when he hears about what happened with his valuable fillies at the truck stop?* she wondered. And there would be no getting away from him. He would probably be staying with Alec in the Coop, the guest cottage by the barn at her family's farm.

Danielle went back to check on the horses and saw Dylan talking to the gray filly, Ninadja. She was Dylan's favorite. The two of them had bonded during the trip in a way Danielle would never have thought possible. Her brother wasn't really a horse person. It was nice to see, she thought.

"Henry Dailey's probably going to be staying at the farm. You know that, don't you, Dylan?" Danielle said.

Dylan nodded. "I figured as much."

Danielle lowered her voice. "I sure hope he's not too grouchy."

Dylan shrugged. "He's meeting us at South Wind, right? We unload the horses, and then we get paid." He rubbed his hands together in mock greed.

Danielle smiled. She hadn't even been thinking about the money now that she had Redman. That made her feel a lot better.

Suddenly, she stopped smiling. *How will Henry react to Redman catching a ride in the van?* she wondered. *Especially after that scene at Aqueduct.* Had Alec told him? She doubted it. But she was also pretty sure that anyone with half a brain could tell that Redman was nothing like Stedman's hyper colt and no threat to the fillies. If anything, Redman had a calming effect on the other horses. At least that's the way it seemed to Danielle.

As they neared Ocala and horse country, Danielle saw a powerful pickup truck pulling a horse trailer pass them. The driver was a woman with high hair and designer sunglasses. She waved at them and Danielle waved back.

Alec turned off the interstate to a local highway.

The scenery was becoming very familiar, with wide green pastures and white fences and horses running around enjoying the early-morning sun. The middle of Florida was about the only part of the entire state that wasn't absolutely flat.

A heavy metal version of "Back in the Saddle Again," a local favorite, was playing on the radio. Sunlight streamed in through the van's side window as trees went by, then a big white house with a faded green peaked roof and a screened-in porch.

"Look, there's One-on-One!" Danielle told her brother excitedly. In front of the house was a sign that read: ONE-ON-ONE TRAINING CENTER—WITH EQUINE SWIMMING POOL. Danielle had been there on a school trip once.

The van drove past golf courses, housing developments, ponds, and small lakes.

"Are you guys all set back there?" Alec said finally.

"We're ready," Dylan answered. *"Definitely* ready."

They were on the outskirts of Wishing Wells now. Danielle saw the familiar hay, straw, and feed store, the tack shop that sold mostly western wear, the pawn and gun shop, the rental equipment shop, and the fast-food pit barbecue. Long dirt driveways threaded through fields of pines and tall oaks draped with Spanish moss.

Danielle wondered if Redman was starting to

ognize the scents of home yet. She hoped so. As they turned into the long driveway that led to South Wind, Danielle could see the barns up ahead and beyond them, a three-quarter-mile training track. She also saw a Shetland pony in the corral, a big satellite-TV dish, three hot-walker turnstiles, and two six-door starting gates on wheels. It was horse-training heaven.

Redman and the other horses in the van seemed to smell the South Wind horses. Ninadja was acting up a little, pawing at the sawdust on the floor.

They pulled up to the receiving barn, and Alec switched off the van's engine. "Well, gang, we made it. Congratulations!" he said. "Get out and stretch your legs." Danielle and Dylan scrambled to be the first to jump out of the van.

Danielle rubbed her eyes, then stretched her arms high over her head. Through the fog in her brain, she could hear birds chirping in the morning sunshine and the neighs of the horses in the nearer barns.

A pair of exercise riders were making their way to the training track, where small groups of horses were getting their morning workouts. From beyond the fence, Danielle heard the drumming of hooves and the slow blowing sounds of galloping horses. It was great to be home.

"Where's Henry?" Alec asked, glancing around. "We have to get these horses unloaded." As he walked to the back of the van, the old trainer approached from one of the other barns, looking as grumpy as usual.

Here comes trouble, Danielle thought.

❧ CHAPTER FIFTEEN ❧

Home

"Howdy, Henry!" Alec called cheerfully. "Guess who I just saw on the way?"

Henry grunted and barely shrugged.

"Oggie Vargas," Alec told him, with a big grin. "You wouldn't believe it. He's riding this big Harley-Davidson motorcycle now."

A mischievous gleam sparked in Henry's eyes. "Oggie? You don't say! Where?"

"He passed us on his bike back in Georgia. He's on his way to Daytona, I think. He said he might stop by later."

Henry shook his head, chuckling as if remembering some good time they'd had together. "He better not come riding up here on any noisy, stinkin' ol' motorbike and scare my horses," he said, roughly but not very seriously.

Alec and Henry immediately began getting the van ready to unload the horses. Unfortunately,

Henry's good mood lasted about two seconds. When he heard about what happened at the truck stop the night before, he got hopping mad. Danielle and Dylan couldn't help but overhear the trainer and jockey exchanging words inside the van. Danielle shuddered.

"What did I tell you about those punks?" Henry said angrily. "You shouldn't even have been stopping at a place like that, Alec. Darn kids."

"Give me a break, Henry," Alec said. "It wasn't their fault. I would have been stopping to eat somewhere anyway. Blame me if you want to blame someone. *I* was the guy who fell asleep, remember?"

Henry harrumphed. "And what's with the paint?"

"That's Danielle's horse. There was room, Henry, that's all," Alec said.

"So we're running a charity horse-transportation company now?"

"Come on, Henry." Alec sounded very tired all of a sudden.

Danielle couldn't stand it any longer. She stepped into the van and headed straight up between the stalls to where Alec and Henry were standing.

"Listen, Mr. Dailey," she said bravely, "I heard what you said about Redman and...well, sir, I don't want you to think I don't appreciate what you and

Alec have done. I mean, helping me get together with my horse again. At least for a little while." Danielle was trying to sound strong, but the words weren't coming out very well. "Anyway, I'll be happy to give up my pay for this job in exchange for Redman's transportation costs."

Henry looked Danielle up and down. "You do understand, miss," he said sternly, "that this is a business we're talking about here? What happened at that truck stop could have been disastrous. These are potentially million-dollar animals."

Danielle nodded politely. *That had nothing to do with Redman,* she wanted to say. But she didn't.

Henry shook his head and sighed. "Fine," he said wearily. "What's done is done. Now get that paint of yours away from my fillies."

Danielle nodded and did as the trainer said. Henry seemed to be ignoring the fact that Redman had been in the same van as his fillies for the past sixteen hours and there hadn't been any trouble at all. Redman had been the most agreeable traveling companion another horse could ask for. His even temper and good example had helped to calm more than one jumpy filly in the past few hours.

"We'll be out of here as soon as he's unloaded," she assured the trainer. "I can walk him home from here. It's only a couple of miles, and we have a lot of catching up to do."

The stern look in Henry's eyes seem to soften slightly. Or maybe he realized that the best thing for him to do was to get back to work. Soon, with the help of a small army of South Wind grooms, he and Alec had the situation well under control.

Danielle watched as they led the tall, leggy beauties away. The fillies looked almost regal in their new coolers and stable sheets. They were sniffing the air and whinnying to the other horses. Darsky jumped around a bit, showing off. They seemed to be in great shape, Danielle thought. Maybe they'd enjoyed all the excitement of their trip. Or perhaps they were just happy to be in a warmer climate. They looked nearly as fresh as they had when they left Aqueduct racetrack…was it *yesterday?*

Danielle rubbed her sleepy eyes again. She still couldn't believe so much could have happened so quickly. It seemed as if they'd been gone a month.

By the time she and Dylan had Redman out of the van, Henry was in much better spirits. He seemed satisfied that his horses were fine despite their late-night adventure at the Seville truck stop.

Alec came over to Danielle and Redman. "You go on now, Danielle. Dylan can catch a ride with me."

"I wish I could see Raven," Danielle said. "He's here, isn't he?"

"Yeah," Alec said, then glanced in Henry's direction. "We'll do that another time, okay? You can spend some time with Redman, catching up."

Danielle nodded and clucked softly to her horse, leading him up the long driveway. They were only a few miles from the farm, so even at a walk they would be home in an hour.

She gave Redman's neck a pat, and together they wandered sleepily off into the morning sunshine.

They had two whole weeks to be together. And they were going to make every minute count.

Have you read all the

YOUNG BLACK STALLION

books?

#1: *The Promise*

#2: *A Horse Called Raven*

#3: *The Homecoming*

#4: *Wild Spirit*

And coming soon:

#5: *The Yearling (August 1999)*

#6: *Hard Lessons (December 1999)*

About the Author

Steven Farley is the son of the late Walter Farley, the man who started the tradition with the best-loved horse story of all time, *The Black Stallion.*

A freelance writer based in Manhattan, Steven Farley travels frequently, especially to places where he can enjoy riding, diving, and surfing. Along with the *Young Black Stallion* series, Mr. Farley has written *The Black Stallion's Shadow, The Black Stallion's Steeplechaser,* and *The Young Black Stallion,* a collaborative effort with his father.